Faerie Kin Files:

Hawthorn Wordsmiths

A.R. Sprouse

Godspeed
Creative
Media

Faerie Kin Files:
Hawthorn Wordsmiths

To My Parents For Always Reminding Me:

Your dragon and knights can live forever and so can the little girl. Never lose your imagination. Never lose the wonder and magic of the world. Never forget to go and visit Puff regularly; then tell the world about those visits. Let the "Jackies" (male and female) of the world be reminded of better days when Noble kings and princes would bow whene'er they came. Give to them a chance once again to revel in the mystic and mystery; to be in a world with no bounds or bonds; to break the captive chains of monotony and triteness; to allow them to soar as captain of their destiny and a peasant to no one.

(Excerpt from a letter from my Father and my commision for my life)

Contents

Department of Magical Phenomenon Surveyance

Faerie Kin File 510260

Mrs. Williams
Creative Writing Assignment
5/18/14

Constance Peters
5th Period
Senior English

How I Became Apprentice To The Witch of Hawthorn Heights

I found her leaning back against the railing at the west entry of the pedestrian bridge in Hawthorn Park. Her hands shoved deep in the pockets of her well-worn jeans, the young woman retreated from the ice-tinged autumn winds beneath her grey, tattered, hoodie; gazing at the world with great disinterest. When Barron had recommended I seek out someone called a Wordsmith, I was expecting . . . well . . . I guess something more magical or at the very least memorable. The drably dressed woman, who almost blended in with the grey of the crisp, November day was easily overlooked next to the ornate wrought-iron pedestrian bridge that spanned the Avalon River.

Hesitating under one of the old-fashioned lampposts that decorated the whole of Hawthorn Park, I debated with myself about approaching the unassuming woman who was supposed to be a Wordsmith. Recalling the saddened and dismayed look on my boss Barron's face at the Hawthorn Recreational Center the day before, I summoned my resolve and made my approach. As I drew closer to the supposed Wordsmith, she made no indication of acknowledging my presence. It was only after I had paused for an uncomfortable amount of time in her close proximity that she merely shifted her eyes in my direction.

"Are you Pippa Hawthorn?" I stammered.

Her reply was the raising of her eyebrows.

"Barron sent me."

I thought I saw a smirk tug at one corner of her mouth, but it disappeared so quickly I could have been mistaken. I fumbled in my jacket pocket for my phone and clumsily pulled up the text Barron had sent me that morning. It had an odd photograph attached. I am still not entirely certain what it was.

3

"Barron told me you could give me something to deal with . . . well . . . some people who are . . . giving me problems."

The Wordsmith finally straightened and stretched before facing me. Her eyes began subtly flitting as she seemed to calculate the sum of my soul.

"Well, you are a bit vague. First used in the French language; derived from the Latin *vagus* meaning 'wandering or uncertain'."

The Wordsmith's last words were spoken almost to herself, but they still struck me as so odd I couldn't find words for any manner of reply. I was flabbergasted by how uncomfortably precise her mumbled words rang in my being.

The woman named Pippa reached down and picked up an old-fashioned tool box, like the ones in western movies, I had failed to notice before. Walking past me across the bridge, she said not another word. I assumed she meant for me to follow her. After silently traversing more than half of the expansive park that spanned the distance between the modern bustle of Hawthorn City and its historic district, Hawthorn Heights, I began to wonder if I had assumed wrongly. The Wordsmith seemed more interested in the fiery autumn foliage than me.

"You have a name, I presume."

I was so lost in my own thoughts I almost didn't hear her to reply, "Constance."

Pippa stopped and assessed me again. The first recognizable expression she had given me that day appeared as a smile slowly spreading across her lips just before she threw her head back in hearty laughter.

I felt uncomfortable. I've always been conscious of how old-fashioned my name is; something others

4

reminded me on a consistent basis. I scowled at the Wordsmith until she managed to contain her laughter.

"How ironic," Pippa sighed, wiping tears from her eyes. "First appearing in the mid- seventeenth century. Derived from the Greek, *eirõneia*, becoming *eirõnikos*, meaning 'dissembling or feigned ignorance'. Though I would lean toward dissemble- first found in late Middle English from the Latin, *dissimulare*, meaning 'disguise, conceal'."

"What?"

"Your name and your current state of mind are at odds. Constance is a Latin name from the word *Constania* meaning 'firm of purpose'. When I first assessed you, I said you to be . . ."

"Vague. Um...wandering...and... mmmm... uncertain?"

"Exactly! From 'exact'. Middle English with a Latin root... oh, well originally a combination of *ex* meaning 'thoroughly' and *agere* meaning 'perform'. Permutation *exigere* meaning 'completed, ascertained, enforced' or *exactus* meaning 'precise'."

Given Pippa's unorthodox manner of speech, I decided that if a Wordsmith could only hold conversations as a dictionary personified, I was glad she didn't speak frequently.

"That would be a dictionary of etymology personified, actually."

I just stared at Pippa in disbelief which must have read as confused for she continued.

"Know you not of etymology, the study of the origin and evolution of words? Origin. Early sixteenth-century French from the Latin *origo* or *origin*- stemming from *oriri* meaning 'to rise'. The rising of words is a much more apt way of phrasing it."

5

"How did you know what I was thinking?"

"Well, how to put it? I can see the aura of the words in your mind."

The word 'aura' made me acutely aware of my surroundings. We were on the avenue leading to the old Hawthorn Estate, a well-known haunt of the Witch of Hawthorn Heights. I began to seriously second guess my going with this strange woman out of a public place.

"Curse that word 'witch'! The English language decides to be original for once and it invented a word that has given us Wordsmiths nothing but grief. Granted, the concept is far older than that particular word. If you are wondering where we are going, we are going to my home. Home. A word from Old English I rather like, having Germanic roots and Dutch relations. We are almost there."

Nearing the huge estate house that had burned out almost a century before, reportedly in a lover's quarrel turned violent, made me anxious. The legend goes that a husband refused to leave his wife for a beautiful witch that lived in the area. The witch cursed the couple and they became so insanely jealous of their spouse that they ended up killing each other.

As part of the curse, the two lovers still haunt the old burned-out mansion, luring in young people to make one another jealous. The jealous spirit would then kill the young person drawn into the middle of the eternal lover's spat in any number of horrific ways. It was also said that the witch regretted her actions and goes to the estate every night to mourn her lost lover. They say she can be heard whispering curses in the dark on anyone who gets too close to her. So there are two very frightening reasons not to venture near the Hawthorn Estate.

To my great relief, we diverged from the main

thoroughfare leading to the estate and onto a smaller path. As we turned, I thought I saw Pippa roll her eyes. The lane we turned onto was once graveled and wide enough for a single vehicle. The two-story rhododendron growing on either side of the path, added to the fact I was following behind someone who could read minds and was carrying an antique toolbox full of any number of murder weapons, made the journey feel claustrophobic.

"If I wished you any harm, I would not lead you into the woods to simply kill your body with rudimentary hand tools. I would crush your spirit in front of the multitudes driving you to take your own life or live in misery."

Pippa's stride remained constant as she spoke without looking back. Just how much of my mind could she read?

Two ancient hawthorn trees stood guard at the end of the hedgerow over the entrance to a spacious meadow. Pippa jumped the old, wooden gate that spanned the opening at the end of the lane with the grace of one who had jumped the fence her entire life. When I hesitated to follow her lead, she opened the gate for me.

In the center of the meadow stood a large, stone building that reminded me of the carriage house in the historic town we visited with grandma the previous year. This one was rather ostentatious by the standards I had seen. Turrets rounded the four corners of the building; each having stained-glass windows in a spiral progression upward. The large, upper hayloft opening had been transformed into an awe-inspiring picture window.

Serving as the main entry of the carriage house, the middle of three carriage doors had become a masterpiece of wrought iron, wood, and glass. Bookending the main entry, the other two carriage doors' upper panes had been turned into picture windows bordered with stained glass flourishes. Below them grew a wild tangle of roses that continued to climb up the building's edifice around the windows. It was like a scene out of a fairy tale... right up till you saw the old, beat-up Range Rover parked to one side of the building.

As impressive as the transformed carriage house was, it was the atmosphere within the meadow that captivated me most. At the risk of being cliche, the air was clearer and sweeter; the colors were brighter; the simple sound of the wind sighing in the last of the fall foliage; and the running of an unseen brook was enough to enchant my soul. I stood, speechless, taking in the beauty that surrounded me. In my peripheral vision I could see Pippa watching me, amused.

A soft nicker finally drew my attention to the left of the house where there was a smaller barn with a paddock. A sense of pure joy filled my being as I looked to see a magnificent, silver dapple charger; with a charcoal, satin coat and billowing, silky, cream mane and fetlocks. Towering over the paddock railing, the stallion seemed eager for attention. Pippa gave me a quick look and a smile.

"So you love horses."

"I have always loved horses. Ever since I was little. But having a horse in Hawthorn City isn't really possible and we could never afford the riding school fees in Hawthorn Heights."

"Well, then let me introduce you to Raijin."

Pippa walked over to the exquisite creature and he lowered his head for her to scratch behind his ears.

"You are lonely, aren't you Raijin? Matilda and Nerida left you by yourself?"

The old-fashioned name struck a sour chord in me. At least Pippa only gave such a name as Matilda to a horse.

"Of course I would name her Matilda. It is a name of Germanic roots meaning 'strength or might in battle'. If you had tried to deal with her as she was when she came here, you would understand. It would seem that my mares have gone off to a far pasture. Raijin here has an abscessed hoof and has to be kept in the paddock till it clears. Abscess. Mid-sixteenth century. Latin base *abscessus*- going away from. As in infected matter being pulled away from the body and collected in a single location via puss."

"Ew."

"I concur it is a word with a rather acrid aura. Raijin, I believe I have a new friend for you to meet. Raijin, this is Constance. Well, come on Constance, you can't give him a proper greeting standing all the way over there."

I practically skipped the distance from the meadow gate to the paddock. Brushing my hand over the velvet of Raijin's nose, I breathed deeply the aroma that reminded me of better days; of days before we had to move to Hawthorn City. For a single instant I was filled with more happiness than I had experienced in a long time.

Pippa gave me a huge smile and allowed me space to dominate Raijin's attention.

"Now there are some healthy auras."

As I scratched behind the horse's ear I couldn't help but ask, "What do you mean words have auras?"

"Aura. Late Middle English. Originating in the Greek as, well, *aura*, meaning 'breeze, breath'. Honestly there are many words I could use to describe the life-force of words; chi, energy, feeling."

Raijin had started to sniff around my pockets. I wished I had an apple for him. "You make it sound as if words are alive."

"They have both a presence and power. But that is too

9

long an explanation for outside in this weather. Shall we go in?"

I desperately wanted to stay with Raijin, but I had followed Pippa for a reason. Though in that moment, the reason didn't seem to be as pressing. Pippa went around to the side of the building and I trotted after her, rounding the corner just in time to see her slip into a lesser impressive wooden and wrought iron door.

A pair of rather substantial thuds could be heard as Pippa shed her heavy, steel-toed work boots. She wriggled out of her tattered hoodie and threw it in an obliging laundry basket sitting next to her toolbox on a large, rough wood table. I stood taking in the iridescent blue of the slate floor and the warmth of the wood cabinets and furniture in the room that doubled as a laundry room and mudroom. A chill breeze stirring a rouge wisp of hair reminded me to close the door.

"Don't worry about your shoes. I just couldn't stand those clunky things any longer. Clunky- first used in 1965. A mere infant in the realm of words."

As Pippa spoke, she traded her obviously sweat-sticky work socks for a pair of brightly- colored fluffy socks and slipped her feet into some very comfortable-looking slippers.

"You can leave your coat and book-bag on the hook if you like."

I quickly complied with the Wordsmith's suggestion and followed her through the door into the rest of the house. Upon entering the main part of the house, I was first overwhelmed by the scent of old books and spiced apple. Clanking and creaking drew my attention to a kitchen that could have been the set for a Jane Austen movie; right down to the woodfire stove into which Pippa was chucking more wood. If there were any modern conveniences in that kitchen they were cleverly concealed.

I wandered into the middle of the room that occupied the vast majority of the space defined by two carriage doors. The slate from the laundry room (which did have a modern washing machine and dryer) continued into the main floor of the house. Dividing the expansive open floor plan down the center was a fireplace large enough to contain a bonfire. Its surrounding stone structure that rose to the second-story ceiling was adorned on both the side opposite and the side facing the grand entrance with what looked like a massive, bronze family crest. The crest featured a tree with one side surrounded by mythical creatures and the other with common animals.

On the side fireplace, opposite the grand entrance, a large set of french doors framed with stained glass looked out on an exquisite garden. Inside, from floor to ceiling, bookcases and curio cases took up nearly every solid wall. The furnishings looked antique yet not uncomfortable- like my grandmother's antique settee. The entire place was magical and rather cluttered with odd things from all over the world.

Ringing the entire width and breadth of the Carriage House, the floor of the old hay loft had been cut to create a broad, rectangular balcony that was accessible by stone spiral staircases in the left turrets and a grand staircase off to the right. The area defined by the third carriage door was closed off with the only door being in the recess under the grand staircase. I assumed that is where the bedroom (and hopefully a bathroom) would be.

"If you need to use the restroom, there is one just off the laundry room!"

Catching myself chuckling, I realized I was growing accustomed to Pippa's outbursts in response to my

11

thoughts as well as her affinity for spouting etymological facts regarding a word from almost anything she would say. Perhaps it was due to the fact that within the context of the Carriage House, Pippa seemed so natural.

Absorbed in my exploration of the first floor, I almost stepped on a large throw pillow that reminded me of a gunmetal-grey, fur haystack. Instinctively, I reached down to pick it up when it hopped away from me. I yelped and jumped back with so much force I nearly overturned the statue behind me.

Pippa poked her head over the bar to see what was going on; her messy bun slipping further out of its confines in the process. "Oh, I see you've met Chaucer the Canterbury Bunny. He is getting a bit grumpy in his old age, but he is harmless."

Chaucer had stopped hopping away and turned to stare at me. Against the tufts of fur I managed to make out ears and his ever-moving pink nose.

"That thing is a rabbit? It's huge and freakishly furry!"

"He is an angora. Turkish- one of the oldest domesticated breeds of rabbit first kept in Ankara, Turkey also known as Angora. There should be a butterscotch, giant French lop around here somewhere named Beatrix. If she hasn't snuck out again, she is most likely upstairs, which is where we will be heading if you'd like to go on up. Oh, and would you like some wassail?"

"What's wassail?"

"It is like a mulled, spiced apple cider. Oh, no worries, this batch isn't traditional. I don't much fancy a fuzzy head."

"I've never heard of such a thing, but sure. I guess."

"Still so vague, Constance. Well, it surprises me you have never heard of wassail; used in the old English celebration to entice The Apple Man to give them a good apple harvest each year. There's even a song about it:

Wassail! Wassail all over the town!
Our toast it is white and our ale it is brown;
Our bowl it is made of the white maple tree;
With the wassailing-bowl, we'll drink to thee!"

Fully committed to singing her strange song (that I later found out was Gloucestershire Wassail), Pippa lost interest in me and returned to whatever she was doing in the kitchen. I made my way up the winding staircase in one of the turrets; wafting after me was the faint melody of Pippa's song carrying with it odd lyrics about calling to his right ear, toasting her left eye, and praising that person's third toe. The spiraling stained glass matched with the spiral of the stairs and played out a beautiful scene as you progressed upward. The upstairs balcony area was similar in feel to the downstairs, only it was a good deal messier.

Piles of journals, notebooks, books, and even parch-ment were scattered everywhere. It seemed that every flat surface sported at least one empty teacup or mug. I had to tiptoe through a hard-found path from the stairs along the bookcase-lined balcony. It wasn't long before I wished I had taken the grand staircase to the larger open area across the way that served as the cap for the bedroom below. Still, even though caution was needed, I found myself being drawn in by a sundry of bits and bobs ranging from lithographs of ancient world maps to a wooden gadget labeled a 'Do Nuthin'. Nearly forgetting about my surroundings, I came hazardly close to upset-ting the bibliographic heaps more than once.

Miraculously, I made it to the open area without

upsetting a single mound of papers and books. The first thing that caught my eye was the gorgeous mahogany drafting table, well, what I could see of it. It, too, was covered in stacks of paper, stacks of blueprints to be exact. Upon closer inspection, I realized they were the original blueprints for most of Hawthorn Heights.

"Have an interest in architecture?"

I whirled around, taking a couple of blueprints with me. Somehow, I had not heard Pippa coming up to the former hay loft, carrying a tray laden with mugs and a plate of cookies. I scrambled to collect up the blueprints and return them to the drafting table as I stammered, "Um. A little. My dad specializes in the restoration of old homes. Or he did. Before the work dried up and we had to move to Hawthorn City. He works in construction now."

"My great-grandfather and his father before him designed and built most of Hawthorn Heights. In his later years, my grandfather decided that urbanization would threaten the family legacy, so he started buying all the properties back. They are held by a trust and managed by whichever Hawthorn is in residence. At the moment, that would be me."

"So you are landlord for all of Hawthorn Heights?"

"Adroitly summarized. Yes, I am the current landlord of some of the most valuable historic homes in the world. Historic, meaning in this case, an over abundance of work. I've had to learn my way around old, creaky pipes and creepy crawl spaces."

Pippa indicated the blueprint on the top of the heap.

"That's where I was banging around on radiator pipes when Barron rang me about you."

Well, that explained her attire.

"Why don't you just hire someone to fix the houses

for you?"

"Because our on-call handyman retired and the process of hiring anyone into the Hawthorn family company is unduly redundant and tedious. Not worth the headache if I know they aren't the right person for the job. Who knows, maybe the right person is hiding in plain sight. Come on over here to the desk and let's have a chat about why you are here. Chat- Middle English from *chatter*- held to mean imitation. Perhaps we should have a discussion instead. Also Middle English, from the Latin root *discutere*, meaning 'investigate'. Yes indeed, let's investigate how you have come to be having wassail and sorghum cookies in the illusive Hawthorn Carriage House. "

My gut tightened and I felt as if I had lost the ability to swallow. I really didn't wish to discuss- excuse me- investigate all the events that had led up to that moment. I stood in my station next to the drafting table as Pippa set the tray down in the only open space on the enormous desk. The Wordsmith looked around with a puzzled expression.

"On second thought, let us take our business downstairs. I do hate to trouble you, but could you carry down the tray so I can collect some reference materials?"

The tension in my shoulders released, betraying just how nervous I was about what was coming. I nodded my consent to carry the tray downstairs. This time, I opted to take the grand staircase to avoid any accidents involving parchment and spilt wassail. As I was carefully making my way down to the main floor, I heard Pippa's muffled voice call out from behind a pile of journals.

"There is a marble-topped table between the wing-back chairs in front of the fireplace. I was a bit chilled so I lit a fire, hopefully it will be nice and cozy soon! Cozy-

18th century Scots. Oh, how I do love Scots!"

There was indeed a marble-topped side table between the two overstuffed wingback chairs. The tray safely settled on the side table, I chose one of the chairs and sank into its velvet embrace. Without thinking, I kicked off my shoes and tucked my legs beneath me; staring into the roaring fire that brought the scene rendered in glass and metal on the firescreen to life.

I tried some of the wassail; it was indeed similar to spiced apple cider, only the spices weren't quite the same and it left a strong tang on the tongue. I next ventured a sorghum cookie. It reminded me of gingerbread, only richer and instantly addicting. I devoured my first cookie and was on my second before I realized it. I forced my-self to slow down, but I was still finishing up my third cookie and entertaining the idea of a fourth when Pippa came down the stairs carrying a stack of journals and books far taller than herself. It was impressive the way she managed to keep everything balanced as if it were no effort at all.

Her reference materials stashed next to her chair, Pippa flopped down with a relieved sigh. She reached for her mug of wassail and took a long sip before turning her attention to me. "So, how is it that Barron sent you to me?"

My mouth again went dry and even a swig of wassail did nothing to moisten my throat as I croaked out, "Well, he caught me looking at his gun."

"The conceal carry he locks up in the safe while at the rec center?"

I simply nodded. I expected her to continue, but she only regarded me with more interest.

"I . . . he had asked me to put away the money from our recent fundraiser. As I was putting the money in the safe I saw the gun and. . . . I know this may sound crazy, but it just suddenly seemed like an answer to my problems."

"The problems you're having with people at school? Quick point of clarification, if you please. Was the gun an answer for dealing with other people or yourself?"

Though I knew I hadn't mentioned school, it didn't surprise me when she spoke of it. Somehow, knowing that Pippa probably already knew everything made it easier to talk. Still, it is harder to say some things out loud and my voice would only support a mere whisper.

"I don't know."

Once again, there was a catch in my throat, only this time from an unexpected sob. I continued with tears slowly slipping down my face.

"I just can't take it anymore. The leering smug looks. The spiteful comments. The names. Bitch. Slut. And . . . and . . ."

"I can see the rest in your mind. Let's just spare ourselves the noxious atmosphere from their being said aloud. Can you tell me why you were being assailed by such words of blight?"

"It's because of him. Conner is his name. We hadn't been here more than a month before he cornered me during a football game. I'm in the band. I play clarinet. Anyway, it was under the bleachers. He. . . He had been drinking. He gave me a back-handed compliment and tried to kiss me. I slapped him."

I found myself without words. I had never told this story aloud. I was too afraid; it was baring my soul to reveal its greatest shame; if I spoke those words, they would become more real somehow. In the things I'd learned that afternoon from Pippa, I started to wonder if

17

there was some truth to that thought.

My body shaking, the tears wouldn't stop, but I couldn't speak. A gentle pressure on my leg drew my attention to the most adorable, large, terrier-sized, butterscotch-colored, lop-eared rabbit I'd ever seen standing on her hind legs, looking at me. The scene caught me off guard and I felt myself relax despite my distress from sharing my tale. The rabbit continued to stand on her hind legs and again reached out with her front paw to touch my leg.

"Beatrix wants you to pick her up."

As soon as the rabbit was in my lap, she snuggled in close. Between the reassuring warmth of her body next to mine and the silkiness between my fingers as I stroked her fur, I was put at ease and I found I could continue my story.

"He got angry and shoved me against a concrete support pillar where he pinned me. He said 'look here, new girl, if you ever want someone to like you around here you better not be slapping me'. I tried to squirm out from between him and the pillar, but he just pulled me back by my shirt, pulling it untucked. We weren't in our uniforms that game. Just our polos and slacks. His hands were inside my shirt. One was sliding under my bra. The other down to my pants. He said, 'You smell good. Maybe I'll just do you right here', I thought, 'I can't stop him'. I wanted to scream, but somehow, I couldn't. Not that it would have been heard over the crowd. I was terrified and helpless.

Then Connor stopped and pulled me around the support column. He clamped his hand over my mouth and told me if I ever told anyone, I'd be dead. That's when the security guard found us. The security guard just told us, 'you kids shouldn't be down here doing such things on school property' and walked away. I ran out from under the bleachers back to the safety of my clarinet section, completely stunned. I ended up having to run to the restroom because I started to throw up. I went home early from the game. My dad was worried about me, but I told him everything was okay. I mean yeah, I got groped. But I was lucky. I didn't get raped. I've heard much worse stories. Mine wasn't worth getting upset over. It was shortly after that the rumors started. Then came the name calling. The isolation. . . ."

As my voice trailed off into sobs, I buried my face in Beatrix's fur. She didn't seem to mind the wet of my tears and made no indication of wanting to be put down. After some time passed, with the sounds of my crying and the crackle of the fire as the only things to be heard in the Carriage House, I noticed another sound. It was the scratching of a pen on paper. I looked over to see Pippa scribbling furiously. I wondered if I was seeing a Wordsmith in action.

"Your father doesn't know about this."

Her hand never lost its rhythm as she spoke.

"And I know for a fact that Barron hasn't a clue either. He will. . . I believe the more contemporary phrase is 'hit the roof'. I know they will both agree with me that you've been violated- in more than one way- by this Conner. It is worth getting upset."

After a few more lines of writing, Pippa handed the paper over to me. There was a glint in her eye that made me wonder just what the aura of the words in her mind were at that moment. I wasn't sure what to expect from the text on the paper, but I was a bit disappointed that it wasn't some kind of spell in a magical language. It was the etymology for all the abusive things that had been said to me.

19

BITCH: A she dog, or doggess. According to the Dictionary of the Vulgar Tongue, 1811 it is the most offensive appellation that can be given to an English woman, even more provoking than that of whore.
Wordsmith Connotation: A word originally used to demean a woman, relegating her below humanity whose only value is sexual servitude.

SLUT: c.1400, Possibly from the German *Schlutt* ' slovenly woman,' dialectal Swedish *slata* "idle woman'. Also from c.1500 meaning 'of loose character, a bold hussy' later morphing to mean 'a woman who commits sexual acts in a shameful excess'.
Wordsmith Connotation: A word used to induce shame by exaggerating sexual exploits to disempower someone.

SHIT: Literal: From Old English *scitte* 'purging, diarrhea'. Feces- from Latin *faex*, 'dregs'.
Wordsmith Connotation: Piece of shit: being of the lowest regarded materials; considered unsanitary, unsightly, and repulsive.

As the list went on, anger flared inside of me. I didn't really know why, but with every word's origin revealed, my fury grew. It was completely irrational. Somehow, I knew that to be the case, but I didn't care. The anger and hatred poured out of me.

"Is this why Barron sent me to see you? So you could tell me just how bad things are in far more detail than I ever want to know? You don't think I know that I've been referred to as something repulsive with no value or accused of vulgar and excessive sexual exploits? That I didn't know what those words were doing to me? What good is knowing how these words came into being? Am I just supposed to show this list to anyone who calls me a name? Do you think they would care? They'd probably just start using these terms instead. If they didn't just tell me to shut the fu . . . "

"I am going to stop you right there. That is a word that I will not allow to be spoken in my house. It is one of the most violent and destructive words ever to come into existence. It's Wordsmith Connotation? Evoking sexual violence and violation. People use it, I believe the phrase is 'left, right, and center', without a second thought; not knowing the dark energy, both extremely explosive and full of a killing aura, it spills into the air like the ash of a volcano."

"So what? You tell that to anyone and they will just put it on repeat, all the while laughing at you. No one gives a second thought to anything they say. Who cares about how words originate or what they mean? They are just words. People just thoughtlessly repeat what they hear. And the people at school? These people are cruel without reason. I know most of them only bully me because their friends are and they don't want to miss out on the fun. But why do I have to be the source of their fun? Oh, that's right, because of Conner. If the name calling isn't enough, he tries to corner me and harass me every chance he gets. Then he ring leads the others. I hate them all! I just wish they would all leave me alone! I just wish they would all die!"

At some point in my rant, I had moved out of my chair and was standing over Pippa. I found I was out of breath. My energy dropped drastically, but my irritation remained.

"Why aren't you saying anything? Where's the use-less lecture about why I am wrong? I know you have

21

plenty of words to say, so why aren't you saying anything?!?"

"I am trying to figure out what words will neutralize
the explosive auras you just unleashed. But it is clear
that anything I say will only ignite them."

"Whatever!" I huffed as threw myself back into my
chair like a petulant child.

"I made that list to help you understand just what it
was that those students were calling into being when they
spoke those words over you. It is little wonder that your
mind was in a place to see a gun as the answer to your
problems. Those words, they all have what are known as
killing auras. Most people don't know that words have
power and every time they are thought, spoken, or written that power releases an aura that affects humans far
more than they can know. However, we Wordsmiths can
clearly see the effects of words on the human spirit and
mind- for we experience the power of words as tangible.
They release a smell, a feel, a color, a sound- some are
strong enough to take us to our knees. They color the
atmosphere of our spirits as individuals and as communi-
ties. There is a reason some words have become known
as curse words. They lay a curse upon those to whom
they are directed and to those that speak them."

Begrudgingly I looked at the paper one more time.
My eyes flitted over some words on her list that rather
surprised me.

WORTHLESS: devoid of worth. WORTH: Old English
weorþ 'significant, valuable, of value; valued,
appreciated, highly thought-of, deserving, meriting;
honorable, noble, of high rank; suitable for, proper, fit,
capable'.
Wordsmith Connotation: A person having no value or

merit and who is unsuitable to live in society of any kind.
IDIOT: early 14c., 'person so mentally deficient as to be incapable of ordinary reasoning'; also in Middle English 'simple man, uneducated person, layman'.
Wordsmith Connotation: Is the same as the definition.

SHAMEFUL: the embodiment of shame. SHAME: Old English *scamu*, *sceomu*, 'disgraceful, dishonorable, loss of esteem or reputation'. (DISGRACE: Italian *disgraziare,* from *disgrazia* 'misfortune, deformity')
Wordsmith Connotation: A deformed entity without honor whose existence is a misfortune for the world.

UGLY: mid-13c., *uglike* "frightful or horrible in appearance," from a Scandinavian source, such as Old Norse *uggligr* "dreadful, fearful," from *uggr* "fear, apprehension, dread".
Wordsmith Connotation: Having a visage that inspires fear and by extension hatred.

DISAPPOINTMENT: Failing to meet expectations. By extension, FAILURE: from Fail, from Old French *falir,* ' to be lacking, miss, not succeed; run out, come to an end; err, make a mistake; be dying; let down, disappoint'.
Wordsmith Connotation*:* To be lacking in either the eyes of others or oneself such that it makes the heart sick.

The list dragged onward full of insults I would never have considered to be among curse words. "These aren't curse words."

"They may not contain exactly four letters, but I assure you, when evoked improperly, they have a similar effect. And those are just the words with the more volatile auras. It would take me a week to compile a compendium of poisonous word combinations that slowly asphyxiate the soul by telling someone they have too much or too little of a particular quality, i.e. too fat, too slow, or superlative statements like 'your best isn't good enough'. The auras of words range from words of life to words of death. Words that heal and words that harm. It amazes me how flippantly people use such a power without caring about the consequences!"

Pippa paused to take a breath. Her intense passion had caused her to tense up as a cat about to spring after a mouse. Slowly letting out her breath, Pippa relaxed back into her chair.

"Knowing how a word came into being helps us understand the auras we Wordsmiths sense from them. In turn, it allows us to understand the mentality of an individual or a group. Understanding how the auras combine, we can call forth peace from turmoil or the reverse just as easily. Finding the right combination of word auras creates what we call Words of Power. They are the most powerful words for a given situation. Wordsmiths have been creating Words of Power throughout history. Their work can be indirectly seen in the likes of the Magna Carta or the Constitution of the United States. Martin Luther, as well as Martin Luther King Jr., were both incredibly powerful Wordsmiths. And so was Adolf Hitler. Words of Power can change the world for good or ill."

Understanding the depth of Pippa's words was a challenge. Being able to see the aura of words seemed a trivial gift, but Wordsmiths helped shape the whole of history using Words of Power. Trying to grasp a truth of that magnitude was beyond my abilities in my worn-out state (indeed I am still not certain I fully understand the

powers that Wordsmiths wield), so I came back to the
one thing I thought I could understand.

"So Barron sent me here to get Words of Power?"

"That is my understanding."

I felt a spark of hope in the darkness of my soul.

"Well, do have any for me?"

"Yours is a more complicated situation than I think
Barron could have known. Though I will tell you, he
was quite worried about you. He felt bad that he didn't
see signs of distress sooner. But you are good at hiding
things so as not be a burden on others. The right Words
of Power for you . . . well, I am going to have to work on
that for a bit."

I was crestfallen. I knew my expression betrayed my
state of mind, but then again so did my state of mind.
"Oh, don't worry. I will help you. I will work on crafting
the Words of Power you need, just be patient."

"How long do think it will take? I need to get home
soon."

"Oh, I won't get them done today. The Words of
Power you need will take quite a bit of time. You'll have
to come back, I am afraid."

The prospect of coming back to the Carriage House
wasn't all that unpleasant. In fact, it kind of made me
happy. There was just something about the place beyond
the Hawthorn trees that enticed me; a sense that anything
could be possible. My spark of hope ignited into a tiny
flame.

"Then of course there is the method of payment to be
decided and negotiated."

Pippa's matter of fact statement left me in shock.

"Payment?"

"Wordsmiths don't hand out Words of Power for free.
You wouldn't be believed what the Gettysburg Address

25

cost Lincoln."

"I am afraid I don't have any money. I work at the rec center to pay for things I need for school and such. My dad just doesn't have any money to spare between us kids."

"Don't look so disappointed. I said we could negotiate the method of payment. How about this: I need help keeping my stable cleaned out and my horses exercised. And I know you feel I could use the help tidying up the place. Why don't you plan to come work for me a few hours a week? I'm flexible about school events and part-time work schedules."

I was thrilled by the offer. I jumped out of my chair, knocking some mail off the side table as I exclaimed, "Yes. I would love to do that!"

Pippa stood and extended her hand to me.

"Then we have an accord? From early 12th century Old French *acorder*, 'agree, be in harmony'. Ultimately derived from the Latin root *accordare,* literally translating 'to be of one heart or to bring one heart to another'."

"Indeed we are of one heart!"

Shaking Pippa's hand, I had to contain my excitement and not jump up and down as I felt like doing. Our accord struck, Pippa was off searching for something.

"I'll drive you home now. I just need to find my keys."

As Pippa hunted for her keys, I stooped to pick up the mail my exuberance had sent flying. Something about them struck me as odd. They had Pippa's name, but it was the address that made me pause. I knew that address and it wasn't the Carriage House.

"Thanks for picking that up! Are you ready to go?"

My curiosity got the better of me.

"This address. Is it the address of Barron's loft? Are

you two . . ."

"No. We have just seen a lot of, well . . . I don't think hellish would be an inappropriate modifier for our past experiences together. As for why my mail goes to his loft? Let's just say that the truth about Wordsmiths is not widely known for a reason. Words of Power can bring out the unsavory types. Barron agreed it was better if anyone was hunting for me, that they find a Marine with a career the government will swear doesn't exist."

"How did you two meet? Do you know his first name?"

"Well, I can't say that we met while he was on an assignment that didn't exist. And yes, I do know his first name. But I won't tell you. Names are some of the most powerful of words, so when someone entrusts you with theirs, it is better if you don't betray that trust. Do you think my first name is Pippa? Now, if you have any more questions, I will or won't answer them in the car as I take you home."

And that auspicious meeting on a cold, November day was how I became the part-time apprentice to the Witch of Hawthorn Heights. It's been almost two years since that day and I have been working off my debt for my Words of Power ever since. Though Pippa has yet to actually give me any Words of Power, I have gained so much from my time spent at the Carriage House.

I've grown quite skilled at riding, partly from exercising Pippa's horses and partly from training the random, shaggy, malnourished, stray, blood-bay stallion that I found wearily wandering Hawthorn Ringed Land while riding one day. Pippa placed him in my care and she helped me train him. I say train, because that is the only word I know to communicate Pippa's unusual methods.

It was more like the stallion and I had to accept one another. At any rate, I named him Aragorn.

While working for Pippa, I learned Japanese, Latin, and a bit of Greek (it turns out I have an ear for languages). I now know the mythology of the Wordsmiths and the significance of the Hawthorn family name. I can read people by interpreting their tiniest movements into useful information. I learned how to cook on a wood-burning stove; how to gather Chaucer's fur and spin it into wool; what the 'Do 'Nuthin' actually was and how to make one; even how to fence!

I am fairly certain that Pippa is the reason Barron offered to teach me the blend of Krav Maga, Kung Fu, and Aikido he developed. Pippa taught me that even though Barron is a walking wall of muscle, he still has vulnerabilities to be exploited. Though I think defeating Barron is easier for Pippa because she cheats using Babel- the Wordsmith ability to daze or confuse people by influencing and altering the auras of their minds.

If I have played the role of Yenta as well as I think I have, Pippa won't be a Hawthorn in name for much longer. I don't know what took those two so long to realize they were in love. It was obvious to me from the start. Maybe it had to do with the circumstances surrounding Barron and Pippa's first meeting. I can understand if that was the case for a couple of years, but I don't get why they had to drag their feet when they knew how they felt for each other.

It wasn't six months from my first meeting with Pippa that my family was moving into the house designated for the official handyman for the Hawthorn family. (Pippa hadn't exaggerated about the hiring process).

As for Conner? After I got over my fear and anger, I started to see that I wasn't the only one that Conner had harassed. With Pippa's encouragement, I reached out to the others to convince them to go together to report Conner. I set a time to go together and frankly, didn't expect any of the girls to show.

Conner found out about it and he stalked me till I was alone. He tried to pull the same stunt saying, shoving me and yelling, 'You bitch! I'll finish what I started and we'll see what you can do then, you slut'.

Okay, so maybe I wasn't as over my anger as I previously mentioned, because when he did that, I got angry. No. Not angry. Livid. Seething. You would have thought I was a Faerie Kin heir to the Wrath of Achilles.

"How dare you! How dare you tell me I am powerless! Who are you to dictate my worth? For over a year, you have harassed me until I accepted that I would never be known as more than the slut you and everyone else paint me to be. But no more. I know who I am. I know where my worth comes from. And it's not from you or anyone else. You're the powerless one here, because I will never again let you have that kind of power over me! I'm not your victim any more. Resigning myself to the fact you control my identity is all in the past. I am Constance Peters! I am more than capable of defining myself!"

With every sentence I shoved Conner backward with such ferocity that he actually looked scared in the end. He tried to reassert his dominance, but I stopped his incoming blow. Then I mercilessly threw him face first into the concrete; giving him an extra kick for good measure. (I can't tell you how proud Barron was of me for that!) After seeing his fat lip and the black eye from his broken nose, nearly all of Conner's victims came with me to file a report against him. He was expelled and sent for rehabilitation.

29

Life for me changed drastically after that, for I meant what I said about no longer resigning the control of my identity to others. I may have succeeded in giving Conner a sound physical defeat, but it was the mental change in me that was my true victory. In that moment of confrontation it was clear to me that I no longer had to accept any worth or identity others assigned me. Even if I hadn't managed to pull off a sweet evasion that landed Conner nose first on the concrete, his power over my soul was broken. I started living by testing the limits of what I could become rather than accepting limitations I was dictated. In two weeks, I am graduating as Valedictorian. At that time, I'll be turning over my post as Student Council President to my very capable Vice-President. Though, I'll be keeping my crown as Band Queen.

The crux of what truly changed my life dawned on me as I was working on my graduation speech. It was a change in the words I accepted about myself.

VICTIM: From the Latin *victima* 'person or animal killed as a sacrifice'. Taking on the meaning 'the oppression of a person held at the mercy of another person or a situation' in the early eighteenth century. **Wordsmith Connotation**: In the short term, someone recovering from being oppressed or taken advantage of. In the long term, it is the resignation to an identity or reality assigned by an oppressive person or situation. Powerlessness to break free of an oppressed identity.

WORTHLESS: Devoid of worth. WORTH: Old English *weorþ* 'significant, valuable, of value; valued, appreciated, highly thought-of, deserving, meriting; honorable, noble, of high rank; suitable for, proper, fit, capable'.

Wordsmith Connotation: a person having no value or merit and who is unsuitable to live in society of any kind.

HOPELESS: HOPE- Old English *hopian* "expectation of relief or aid, looking forward to a desirable future". Hopeless, by extrapolation from Hope, is 'without expectation of relief or aid, accepting a prolonged suffering and futile future'. **Wordsmith Connotation:** Living according to actions and beliefs that one has no future. Accepting that the current status of life is the only status life can achieve.

ISOLATED: From the Latin *insulatus*, 'made into an island'. By extension, 'cut off from the mainland, difficult to reach or leave'. Often associated with ALONE: From Old English *all ana*, 'wholly+one'; extrapolated meaning, 'the one is the entirety of existence'. **Wordsmith Connotation**: Being cut off either by choice or by force to an existence in which one only has one's own powers to rely upon with no expectation of reinforcement or aid. A state of understanding that one's own powers are insufficient and accepting (often in fear) that should one fail or fall there will be no one to bail them out and they will cease to exist.

REJECTED: From the Latin *re* 'back' + *jacere* 'to throw'. **Wordsmith Connotation:** Deemed by others (and self) as not meeting the acceptable requirements or set standards to merit value. See Worthless.

These were the words Pippa sensed in me when I thought of myself the first time we met. All of the above were combining as the etymology of Constance Peters.

31

It was the acceptance of these words as the truth of who I was that pushed me to a place where a gun seemed like a solution to my problems. Working for and learning from Pippa has helped me to acquire a new vocabulary to define myself.

CAPABLE: Latin *capere* 'ability to take, hold, or grasp'. A bedfellow of, POWER, from Latin *posse*, 'to be able'. **Wordsmith Connotation**: Ease of management regarding a given task. Being able to act with an appropriate and required response over one's responsibility. Being able to accomplish an undertaking.

INTELLIGENT: From the Latin *intellegere*, 'to understand or comprehend'. A trait supported by DISCERNMENT, from DISCERN; originating from the Latin *discernere* 'ability to distinguish one thing from another, perception of what is from what is not'. **Wordsmith Connotation**: Having the ability to put together ideas by seeing how they are correlated with one another; ability to respond with the appropriate words or actions based on what is comprehended; ability to understand the truth about one's self and the world around them; ability to detect and reject what is false.

HOPEFUL: Hope- Old English *hopian* 'expectation of relief or aid, looking forward to a desirable future'. Extrapolation to Hopeful, 'full of expectation of relief or aid, fully looking forward to a desirable future'. **Wordsmith Connotation:** Refusing to accept that current circumstances are the only circumstances that can be expected. Expecting and seeking aid from those around one's self. Living according to actions and beliefs that build toward a future that exceeds the present.

VALUED: From the Latin *valere*, 'possessing strength, worth, and value'. **Wordsmith Connotation**: Appraised as having worth and merit by virtue of exemplary contribution to an individual or a society. Of note: the Appraisers of one's value are both society and the individual; of the two, the most powerful Appraisal is from the individual as they will act and live according to their estimation of themselves.

Pippa never meant to give me Words of Power.

Teaching me to find my own Words of Power had been the Wordsmith's plan all along.

Afterword

I know short stories don't have afterwords, but as I am editing this before turning it in tomorrow, I feel I should warn you about something. This is the only copy of this story and most likely it will disappear soon after you give it a grade- for that is what happens to stories involving people who don't officially exist in this world.

The probability of this assignment going up in smoke has increased since I found out that Pippa and Barron are going off together. They've disappeared before, but this time it is different. Pippa has asked me to move into the Carriage House to look after the place and take care of the animals.

As there must always be a Hawthorn Wordsmith in Hawthorn Heights, Pippa tells me one of her cousins from Great Britain is participating in the exchange program at Hawthorn University, where I will be attending next fall to study linguistics and humanities. He is to live in Barron's loft, so I won't have to worry about forwarding Pippa's mail.

Having met one Hawthorn Wordsmith has lead me on the greatest adventure of my life. I can't help but wonder what life will be like to meet a second Hawthorn Wordsmith. His name is Rhys Hawthorn.

Rhys. Of Welsh origin. Meaning 'ardor'- from the Latin 'ardere', 'to burn'. Often translated to mean either passionate or rash.

Hawthorn. A tree the Celts say stands for duality; often said to be sacred to fairies; that can stand on the threshold of two worlds; whose blossoms grant blessing to young lovers and branches the wood for witches' brooms.

May Quiller
a.k.a Pippa Hawthorn
Substitute Teacher

How I Spent My Summer Vacation In Hell

Barron,

I found this in a stack of papers. You've both given me snippets of your history, but I was wondering if you'd give your side of this story.

Constance

Gehenna. The biblical place known for unspeakable acts of inhumanity such as the sacrifice of children by burning them alive as offerings to Ba'al, Moloch, and company. It is now held to be another name for Hell- a destination for the wicked. Whoever named that black ops base in the Hindu Kush was surprisingly forthcoming in their choice of monikers.

Most people think of Hell as a place of fires. It is my experience however that 'Hell' has an aura of suffering. Late 14th century. From suffer which replaced the Old English *þolian, þrowian*- meaning "undergo, be subject to, be affected by, experience, be acted on by an agent". Subject to what? For me, I feel an almost unbearable agony from the word. Agony. From Old French meaning 'anguish, terror'. When people disappear into a place without official existence, without accountability, they often find themselves in Hell.

Gehenna was a far cry for the paradise I was supposed to be enjoying as my summer vacation. One last hurrah before I officially began my duties as a Wordsmith. Though, as a Hawthorn, I was born doing the duties of a Wordsmith. I was furious when I got the call that the Wordsmith given this assignment was suddenly and inexplicably unavailable for duty and the Faerie Kin Council was sending me in their place (furious, but not in the least bit surprised).

Wordsmiths have always had working relationships with governments. Indeed most governments in the world are in debt to the Wordsmiths and the

Faerie Kin Council. As acts of goodwill, the Council helps with requests from various governments for situations that are best dealt with using the particular gifts of Wordsmiths or other Faerie Kin. Interrogation was a common request and one the Council will grant on a whim if it does not see any benefit to themselves from it. As I had drifted in and out of what passes for sleep on an airplane, I wondered which reason had prompted the granting of this request for a U.S. Joint Intelligence Operations Center and which answer to that question infuriated me more.

A gentle shaking roused me from my limbo of consciousness.

"Miss Pippa, we're landing. Time to get our game faces on."

The rough calloused hand on my shoulder and graveled but gentle voice belonged to the head of my security detail from the Hawthorn Private Security Force, Dane Ford. Dane was an old special forces
operative from a time before what he calls the 'politically correct regime'; giving him more than a few wild stories to tell. Dane had been the head of my protective detail for most of my life. He was more of a grandfather to me than either of my biological ones that I only ever see once every few years. What family he had was lost before I was born. It was Dane who taught me how to fight, how to survive when I shouldn't be able to, and countless other life lessons from how to cook and how to flirt, to how to change the oil in my car.

"Now let's review. I'm the big shot integration

specialist being flown in to determine if the Taliban really has been taken over by a new warlord- accounting for the uptick in terrorist activity. And if there is, who are they and where can we find them. And you . . ."

"Are your assistant and private interpreter, May Quiller. I am not to have any direct contact with those being interrogated. I am to read them from a distance and alert you to anything of significance."

"That's my girl. Trevino, Jacobson- you two keep a close eye on Miss Hawthorn. If you even think you smell trouble I want her on this bird and in the air without delay."

The other two members of my security detail confirmed their orders and started quadruple checking their various weapons. My own shoulder holster chaffed me something awful and I tried to adjust it so that it was more comfortable to no avail. I too pulled my firearm and checked it; partly out of habit and partly to appease Dane who was waiting for me to do so. Even then his eyes lingered on me longer than normal.

An interrogation gig was standard work for a Wordsmith and was usually a matter of going in and out in a couple of hours. But, something was off, or at least Dane thought it was. Though I have never met anyone who could order his own thoughts so precisely to keep even a Wordsmith guessing his true mind, I still knew Dane's tells. The fact that he was taking point as the interrogator meant he didn't trust

anyone knowing I was the specialist that had been called in. He'd been wound more tightly than I'd

41

ever seen him since I had gotten the assignment and his endless mental recitation of poems meant he knew something he didn't want me to know.

As our custom designed aircraft, largely modeled on a military osprey, settled onto the ground, I stood and shook out my slacks; smoothing out any wrinkles and making sure the twin long bladed knives sheathed in the tops of my tall boots did not make a readable impression. Easy accessibility to them under my slacks wouldn't have been a possibility, but Dane insisted I have them. I'd been grateful I hadn't been asked to wear a skirt; the heels on my designer boots were bad enough. I adjusted the modified money belt carrying any number of important personal documents and serving as a sheath for a couple of smaller throwing knives that sat around my waist beneath my shirt.

Slipping into my jacket, I took the same precaution with my shoulder holster as my knives. Being armed was probably a given in a place called Gehenna, but Dane had taught me to never let anyone know for sure just what kind of arms I was carrying until they were at the mercy of them (or preferably, according to Dane, they had died of them). Using my reflection in the window, I double checked my hair was still smoothed in place. When I was certain nothing about my appearance could be misconstrued as anything but generic, I pulled my briefcase from under my seat then trotted back to the cargo hold to take my place next to Dane. Generic. 1670's English from the Latin stem *genus*- kind, stock, race. First taking on the meaning of 'indistinguishable, not name brand, having little memorable impact' around 1977.

Steeling myself for the onslaught of auras I knew was coming, I focused on the slow descent of the cargo hold door. It wasn't that I couldn't already sense the overall mentality of the base, but the osprey was a physical barrier that made it possible for me to separate myself from the minds of those outside. As the welcome party came into view I fought to keep from wincing or tightening my grip around my briefcase handle; anything that could serve as a tell that I was being suddenly asphyxiated by the auras emanating from the occupants of the base.

Military outposts tend to be full of explosive language often carrying killing auras. For a Wordsmith, 'curse words' had come by their name for a reason. But it wasn't the salty language that caused me the most discomfort. There is an unrelenting pressure, an
underlying fear, and an unmitigated anger that weighs on a person's spirit in those kinds of places causing the soul to lash out in language and action that slowly poisons the atmosphere. In short, Gehenna was a pressure cooker of killing auras.

Jacobson and Trevino had been on my detail for a couple of years and they had known full well my feelings; so they marshalled their thoughts and observations to clever quips that had light and airy auras, many of which tickled, in order to help set me at ease. Handpicked and personally trained by Dane, these were not just men who were good at their job, they were good men. I may not have felt safe, but with my security detail I somehow hadn't felt afraid.

A four man welcome party, shielding their eyes from the dust devils whipped up by our rotors, came into view. They had the look of men who had long been away from the world of formal dress parades and spit shined shoes; having a wild and weather worn look that blended them into the landscape more than their camouflage. <u>There was a notable shock at seeing a woman among our party.</u> Beyond that initial shock the language of their thoughts ranged from having the grating and fatiguing auras of being around a pouting child who is put out about being forced to entertain high profile guests (in some cases about those things having to be 'swept under the rug', as it were, because of high profile guests) then coming round to the fresh air smell of auras hopeful that answers might finally be achieved. The language focused on why we were there had anxious auras that were urgent in nature. What Dane had called an 'uptick in terrorist activity' was being addressed in a far more serious manner in the thoughts of the men at Gehenna. If Dane was downplaying that, I had to wonder what else he had downplayed.

"I am glad you could make it, I wasn't sure if you would come," the commanding officer heartily welcomed us, shaking Dane's outstretched hand. "I'm Wells. Don't worry with the honorifics. You won't be here long enough for that if what the top brass tells me is true."

"I am Booker Mayson and this is my assistant and personal interpreter Mary Quinn. These gentlemen are Trevino and Jacobson."

I was shocked by Dane's introduction. The

44

I don't think shock quite covers it. It was more like being hit by lightening. Not only had a woman come to Gehenna but it was a woman who looked like she'd never known hardship. The two should never have met.

change had been a split second decision, but that wasn't what shocked me. Throughout history there have been two cover names used worldwide by Wordsmiths when working with outside groups. In the most recent of history our women are May Quiller and our men are Booker Mayson. Essentially, Dane had introduced himself as the Wordsmith and I knew from his thoughts that he meant to sell it that way to everyone on base. Something about the commanding officer had spooked him.

"We were told to expect private security. This is Barron. He will be assigned to your group while you are here, so don't hesitate to ask him for anything."

Barely aware of the exchange of pleasantries, I had been more taken with my surroundings. Gehenna's base of operations was in a canyon having moved into what appeared to have been a monastery carved out of the mountainside. The only visible ways in or out were our osprey and some goat trails zigzagging up the steep canyon wall. (I knew our pilots had been a credit to the HPSF, but it had been no small feat to land the osprey in the confines of the canyon. I made a note to let the pilots know how impressed I was and that I'd be putting down a glowing report of them in my debriefing later.)

From the outside, the place looked abandoned and forgotten after a seismic event centuries before. The crumbled statues of unknown deities laid claim to my attention as I tried to figure out who would have been committed enough to carve such an impressive structure into the hard stone with naught but hammers and chisels. I also wondered who would have ever thought to turn these tumultuous ruins into a black ops base.

"It's nice to meet you Miss Quinn."

A young man's voice pulled my attention back to its proper place. I snapped my head forward once more and saw that the Marine with helter-skelter, longer-than-regulation hair, and a fair amount of scruff named Barron had extended his hand. I shook it and returned the salutation as movement in my peripheral vision prompted me to quickly fall in behind Dane and Wells who chatted about nothing of any great importance. It was conversation meant to mark time until the pair of them were behind closed doors.

"Please watch your step, Miss Quinn. The canyon floor is full of loose stone."

<u>What the man Barron hadn't said out loud was that my boots were far too impractical for the terrain and I had to agree.</u> The welcoming committee were in combat boots and camouflage that were covered in the grit that layered the canyon despite the telltale signs of the struggle to dust it off. Our expensive silk suits and designer footwear were anything but practical in

Gehenna, but they sold our parts as possible mafia.

Despite his disapproval of my footwear, Barron was kind enough to offer his hand to patiently help me navigate the more tricky terrain as we approached the main temple's caved in entrance. Moving in a close knit pattern to myself and Barron, Trevino and Jacobson simultaneously kept a close eye on us and made mental notes about possible extraction methods. It was a challenge not to roll my

46

eyes when it was clear that throwing me over their shoulders was a favored tactic . . . and they weren't even attempting to be clever.

I paid close attention as we carefully picked our way through the debris that created a labyrinthine path from the temple entrance deeper into the mountain where the natural light faded and the air grew musty. Our guides produced flashlights to help us see the last several yards of the journey. As we emerged into the first open cavern I was struck by a smell I will never forget. It was the smell of gasoline from the generators and kerosene from lamps; unwashed bodies and bodily waste; the smell of blood and disease; the putrid smell of infection and decay.

I fought to keep from covering my nose and mouth with my hand. It wouldn't have helped anyway. I knew that what I was sensing was more about the auras in the place than the actual smell. As I said above,
Gehenna was aptly name. That smell was the aura of unchecked rage, unbridled cruelty, unspeakable terror, and unbearable anguish; it was the aura of Hell.

Despite my best efforts to seem un-phased by my surroundings, I still looked a little green which caused Barron to regard me with concern. I gave him my brightest smile to prove I was alright and made small talk; partially to occupy my mind and partially to gain information no one would ever say out loud.

Being a Wordsmith means having to learn how to lead mental conversation as much as verbal. I asked questions that were innocuous in terms of verbal response but prompted certain lines of thought. Out loud what Barron gave me was a cursory tour of the base, but internally the wording of his thoughts had auras that pricked and cut. Auras that had the sound of metal scraping against metal, so deafening you thought your ears were bleeding, told a riveting tale that explained much about Gehenna and its overwhelming compounded collection of auras.

Once past the collapsed portion of the temple, the open space had been lit with bare bulbs chained together with cables that radiated as spider webs around various generators. What was revealed in the light of the illuminated spider webs was an odd cross between a modern military and traditional gypsy camp. Official business was conducted in adapted military temporary structures. Personal quarters were claimed and created out of small rooms cut into the rock; whatever material was available draped across the entry ways.

Dane and the Wells went into the command tent to talk where there were fewer ears while Barron lead Trevino, Jacobson, and myself to a large canvas tent. The tent served as the entry way for spacious cavern in the wall that had been turned into a canteen. A dozen men sporting the fatigues of various military branches, including a few international ones, looked up as we entered. Curiosity abounded as the mental questions tossed to and fro regarding the overdressed trio
Barron lead to a table in a quiet corner.

Everyone had known outside contractors were coming but I had to focus on keeping a straight face in light of the rather absurd manor of rumors and assumptions that had been made about just who it was that was coming to do interrogations guaranteed to see results. Some of the auras reminded me of a child's looking under the bed with the expectation of finding the boogeyman.

There was again some awe that a woman was in our company, but this time the lines of thought alerted me to more of the hellish history of Gehenna. Predominantly, I sensed the words 'they can't let a woman back there'. The words that followed I've tried to forget to this day, but will never be able to. It was from such thoughts that the aura of Hell's smell grew more pungent. Gehenna lived up to its name for those men in many ways.

Barron, who had stepped away to get us some bottles of water, returned and made note of our assessing sweeps of the canteen. "If you would please, forgive them their rude stares. We've never had a woman in Gehenna. At the risk of sounding politically incorrect, this really isn't a place for women. No offense to
whatever accomplishments you have to your name."

Trevino and Jacobson gave curt nods, but I couldn't help smiling at Barron. There was something about him that reminded me of Dane.

"No offense taken. Most of what I sense in the eyes of these men is concern." To myself I thought, "More for themselves to some degree than me, however."

"I'll go ahead apologize for the wolfish gleams you

most likely sense in their eyes as well. Like I said. . ."

Despite my best efforts not to draw attention to myself, every eye had been immediately drawn to me. I was hit with every manner of aura; from the repugnant odor of the impolite equivalents of 'little missy' to the highflying sense of pleasure followed by male fantasies- of which the demeaning language of some made me want to throw up. Demean. Circa 1600's 'lower in dignity'. Modeled on 'debase', c.1560's. On analogy from the obsolete verb base meaning 'to abuse'.

Dane long ago apologized on behalf of all men for their inability to control where their minds would go in the presence of a woman. However, according to Dane, you can tell the character of a man by how he manages his thoughts after they initially present themselves. For men who willfully prolonged their indulgence in their fantasies, then you judged them by the nature of their fantasies; if violent, then stay as far away as possible and strike first if they get too close; if simply sexual, just keep your guard up and maintain a healthy distance between you. If a man had any inclination that he might ought keep his fantasies in check, then you could most likely trust him for he has some sense of deep character and moral center. If I met a man who actively tried to control his thoughts and fantasies, I was to bring him to Dane for an interview for marriage candidacy. Perhaps his exact words were, 'such a man is worthy of your trust', but I knew Dane's thoughts all too clearly.

Barron had captured my attention because he fell into the category of a man I could trust. Making

I remember that suit you wore. It was tailored to fit al of your curves. Not that I am excusing those guys. You've got another one you insist on wearing on assignment I am thinking should go the way of that dark blue dress that draped low in the front, had a low back and showed off your legs

You said the cleaners lost that dress!

50

an ally of him was important so I made a show of assessing
Barron's words and my giving the weight and importance that he wanted them to have.

"A woman has never been in Gehenna. I get that. What accomplishments I may be able to boast would be modest, but I am obviously not unaccustomed to being the only woman among men. But there is something more on your mind than what discomfort I may be experiencing from your comrades."

"That man Booker said you were his interpreter. Does that mean you will present for the interrogations?"

"Booker knows I need to be on hand for the interrogations, but I believe it is his wish that my presence not be known to those being interrogated. Mr. Barron, I can see your concern is genuine. I am not here by accident. I was born to this line of work. There is more to me than I may. . . um. . . seem."

I hadn't meant to falter in my speech, but I had felt it. I knew I had sensed an aura projecting an accurate image of standing at the border of the Twin Worlds; surrounded by the melodic hum of magic; accompanied by the sensations of apprehension and respect; the aura often associated with Wordsmith. I turned my attention to hunting the source of the reference, but all related thought was lost as suddenly as it had surfaced. I knew my hesitation had not escaped the notice of our babysitter and was relieved when another man sat down across the table from us. It was subtle, but I felt Trevino and Jacobson bristle.

"What's this I hear about me being replaced as interpreter?" The man's voice was thick with a southern drawl and his fair features could have easily been featured on a fashion magazine. "What wasn't I pretty enough?"

"You've got the prettiest mug in Gehenna and you won't let anyone forget it, Nottingham. This is Jacobson, Trevino, and Miss Mary Quinn. This good old boy is Nottingham."

"As in the forest. . ."

I couldn't stop myself from quipping, "I think you mean the sheriff."

Nottingham stood and gave a comical bow. "I fancy myself more of Robin Hood than the sheriff if you please fair Maid Mary."

I laughed, mostly because I knew it was what Nottingham was hoping to achieve. He was the kind of man that hid his thoughts even from himself in jokes and sarcasm. <u>It was a kindness that cost me nothing to give him a reason to wear a genuine smile.</u> It was worth it, his eyes sparkled and his smile was undeniably dashing

"Laying it on a bit thick aren't we Robin Hood?"

"Now listen here Barron, you've already got a wife and a child on the way. On top of that you are due to go home day after tomorrow so you'll have the opportunity to charm as many women as you like. I've got to make the most of this golden opportunity."

Barron jerked his thumb in the direction of Jacobson and Trevino who had been visibly less than amused by Nottingham's antics. "I am fairly certain your golden opportunity has guard dogs that won't

52

Nottingham had 5 sisters. To hear him tell it they were all hellcats. But he never stopped talking about them. Trust me your small kindness was huge for him.

hesitate to bite."

Trevino and Jacobson's cleverly crafted mental responses made me giggle sparking a pleased gleam in their eyes. Nottingham seemed to think it was he who had made me giggle and would have continued his buffoonery (16th century French for clown. Though originally contributed to an old rare Scots word that came to mean a professional jester. Oh, how I do love Scots!) had not Dane and Wells entered the canteen bringing everyone to attention. Whatever they had been discussing hadn't taken long. My honor guard and I rose and went to meet Dane.

"Let's not waste any more time and get down to business," Dane ordered, leading us directly out of the canteen.

Wells hurriedly caught up to Dane and Nottingham and Barron followed close behind us. Many different thoughts also trailed after us as we were lead down a long narrow stone passageway. Auras that were suffocating, wild, numb, disparate, with maniacally unhinged overtones grew stronger. I knew we were getting closer to where the prisoners of Gehenna were being held. We pulled up short of a long row of pits and went to a set of smaller carved out rooms outfitted for interrogations. Dane led Trevino, Jacobson and myself into one of them. Barron followed us, but Wells and Nottingham went into the one next door.

"Miss Quinn, you should be able to hear us well enough from in here. We'll communicate via our comlinks. You hear anything you think their interpreter missed, let me know."

I nodded my compliance to his orders. Something nagged at the back of my mind and I pulled
Dane over away from Barron's ears. "Did Wells happen to use the term Wordsmith while you were with
him?"

A mild concern read on Dane's face. "No. But I
suspect he is no stranger to the term. Why?"

"Because I am certain I heard someone mention
a Wordsmith while we were in the canteen. It was
brief and faint, but it is not something I could mistake."

Dane looked grim. "Trevino, go back out and
check on the plane."

Trevino left without a word to attend to his
coded instructions and I could see Barron was torn
between staying with us and following after Trevino.

"Jacobson, you stay with Miss Quinn. I can handle the interrogation on my own. You know your
orders from here."

On his way out of our little interrogation alcove,
Dane stopped and offered his hand to Barron. "You
are a good man Barron. I entrust you to keep us all
safe and well looked after."

Barron looked more than a little bewildered, but
he accepted Dane's hand.

Five minutes later the interrogation began. The
first thing I noticed was that Nottingham was a
completely different man in the interrogation room.
It wasn't a complete surprise, but the cold lifeless
husk filled with enmity was so unlike the lively man

I'd met in the canteen it was eerie. In many ways the auras of his thoughts toward the prisoner stripped both men of their humanity.

I wrapped my arms around myself trying to calm the tremors I felt beneath my skin. Being in a position to observe two men on opposite sides of a conflict simultaneously, I was fully aware that their thoughts mirrored one another; each held different convictions of a similar ilk that had lead them there; each had experiences that taught them to think the way they did. It hit me hard why part of the Wordsmith Connotation of War is an infectious inhumanity.

I forced myself to attend to the thoughts of the man being interrogated. Words have power no matter what the language and they embody the same auras no matter how they are pronounced. Still, I had to carefully attend to the precise language of the man's mind so as to be able to feed leading questions to Dane.

I cleared two men in 30 minutes. They truly had no information to offer on the subject of our interrogation, but there was something oddly similar to their lines of thought that left me rather unsettled. When I encountered it again in the third I decided to pursue the oddities with an unorthodox line of questions for Dane to ask.

"Ask him how he came to be here. No, ask him why he is still here."

Barron would give me odd looks when I would suggest questions to Dane that didn't seem to make any sense to ask. Whatever was going through his mind I had to ignore so as to sense every aura, no

What was going through my mind was that you were the most bizarre interpreter I'd ever met. Even then I knew you weren't listening to the prisoner's words. It was like you were hunting something

Bizarre is a much 55 kinder term than I'd have guessed

matter how small, from everyone in the interrogation room. Indulging my hunch paid off as my question triggered something in the man's thoughts. I felt a tantalizing aura that is similar to the smell of fresh out of the oven cookies tinged with the sensation you get when you stand too close to a live wire; the aura for 'bait'.

"Ask him what reward he will receive for his bravery."

I honestly didn't care about the man's response to that question; I already knew what to expect and he did not disappoint. You can't hurry anyone when leading them along a line of thought. They have to feel safe enough to believe that their thoughts are going in a direction they have chosen.

"Ask him what he thinks he has done to deserve that kind of reward."

It took a minute to sort through the various auras the man's mind was expelling, but I once again felt the sensation of the aura for bait. Close by it was the aura for magic; not like a child's understanding of magic with sparkles and wonderment; it was the most common reaction to the idea of magic being real the world over- fear and suspicion, panic and condemnation.

It was my turn to choose my words wisely. "They are Pollywog jigs."

Jig. Mid 16th century of unknown origin. Meaning many things including a type of lure used by jerking it about in the water. Pollywog. The embarrassingly persistent code name used by Dane derived from my childhood nickname Princess Pippa Pollywog.

Constance! What have you done!

56

Jacobson was by my side in an instant; my arm securely in his grasp as he pulled me toward the exit. It was the first time I'd noticed that Trevino hadn't returned. Barron was baffled and mildly alarmed by Jacobson's sudden change of mannerisms and wary of the bodyguard's drawn weapon. Barron raised his hands in a show of submission and followed us back down the stone passageway toward the temple entrance.

Echoing, I could hear Dane's voice declaring that he wanted to change his tactics for this round of interrogation. I knew he was about to give the man an injection that would paralyze him. Dane then announced that it would take the serum a few minutes to start working, so he wanted to step next door for a second. Nottingham and Wells thought nothing of Dane's words or action and agreed to keep an eye on the prisoner for a few minutes.

Jacobson's pace never slacked and left Dane far behind as my body guard's mind raced with every scenario possible; all while keeping a sharp eye on everyone and everything in Gehenna. Barron's mind was a tempest of conflicting thoughts; every manner of protocol flooded his mind, but his gut told him to stick with me and Jacobson. I was relieved when he chose to go with his gut. Relieve. From the Old French *relever* directly stemming from the Latin *relevare* 'to lighten, to lift up, to liberate from a burden'. A breath of fresh air and the light of hope are the aura of relief.

As for my own mind, I refused any emotions access to my thoughts. The enormity of that circumstance would have crushed me if I had let it fully

I forgot how green you were back then. My gut had told me something was off the moment you lot showed up. And that I was connected to you. I didn't hesitate. You were just too frightened to know the difference.

take a hold of my mind. Every step I took was with full deliberation and every thought in my mind was directed to what I knew had to happen next. It was my job to know what others were thinking so as to give us an advantage.

Despite my best efforts to remain focused I still almost missed the false auras- thoughts that are deliberately crafted so as to keep the true mind of a person concealed. Dane was a master of them. He often used nursery rhymes or poetry to keep the words in his thoughts from betraying his purpose. It was annoying, but it also had taught me how to detect false auras; and once I detected them in Gehenna, I was stunned by the sheer number of them. Several people were deliberately generating false auras.

Fully relying on Jacobson to guide me, I had been paying no mind to where my feet were going. It is a testament to his skill that we didn't trip over a single obstacle till there was one in the murkily lit maze passage to the temple entrance. What tripped us was a leg. Though we both managed to regain our footing what I saw next dropped me to my knees. The leg belonged to Trevino who was a bloodied mess and whose mind was quickly evaporating from this realm.

Scrambling I checked his pulse and he feebly pulled my hand away from his neck, placing it on the backpack he was clutching. His voice was barely audible and the there was a sharp wheeze between words.

"F...fffor you. . . lost com . . . flight cccc. . . ccrew dead . . . been honor . . . miss. . . Pip. . .pa."

To my horror Trevino's hand went limp; his mind went dark and silent indicating his soul had vanished. Panic unlike any I had ever felt before restricted my breathing and nearly sent my whole body into convulsions. Strong arms surrounded me and pulled me up from the ground and into a deep shadow.

"Quiet. Someone's coming."

Hugging the backpack I'd managed to keep a hold of, I combated the overwhelming fear and pain so I could focus on the mind of the one whose footsteps were quickly ticking through the entrance maze. To my great relief, it was Dane.

Feeling me relax in his grasp, Barron loosened his hold. Pulling his sidearm the Marine placed himself in front of me. The briefest flash in the shadows across the way and some carefully selected words alerted me to Jacobson's location. As Dane came into view with his own weapon pulled, I had been certain that Barron and Dane were going to shoot one another. Instead they had a standoff as each tried to take the full
measure of the other.

"You okay Miss Pippa?"

"Yes, but Trevino."

"So flying out of here isn't an option. Son you are either with us or against us; meaning you are either going to help us find another way out of here or I will drop you where you are."

Barron's gaze went from me, to Dane, to Jacobson, back to me. His thoughts clearly indicated he wanted an explanation. I quickly sorted through several word combinations to find the most succinct

59

I accidentally got between a tiger & her cub once. She was a kitten compared to that old man. Seriously, Dane Ford is terrifying. He meant it when he'd said he drop me without a thought.

way to explain.

"Someone went to a great deal of trouble to lure us here."

"Why? Who are you?"

"We'll answer what questions we can, but not while we're sitting ducks on a killing field."

Dane's answer momentarily satisfied Barron's curiosity and he took point leading us back the way we had come, this time with a few new turns that led us out into a different part of the monastery. We ducked in and out around rock formations that ringed an open space until we came to a place where a faint breeze could be felt.

"There is a tunnel out back there. Now I want some answers."

"Pippa. You know what you need to do. I need to have a discussion with this young man."

Dane took Barron aside and started to give a brief explanation. In the time it took Dane to relay that idea that I was a Wordsmith (which he translated as psychic for expediency) and that if I was caught I'd be enslaved, I'd opened the backpack Trevino had given me. I pulled out the flowing black robe that I slipped over my clothes; broke the heels off my boots; got out of my slacks and into the more sturdy cargo pants from the backpack; pulled the boot modifications over my boots and new pants, adjusted the sheaths for my knives; situated my shoulder holster over the first robe and under a second; and was in the process of winding a cloth around my waist with another in my hand to wrap over my head as a hijab. <u>Barron was clearly taken off guard by my quick change when he and Dane</u>

60

<u>turned to return to me.</u>

Up to that point I had assumed that Jacobson had taken the rear and had been behind us the whole time. I was shocked when he came running up to us carrying a second backpack (that I think Trevino may have been carrying at one point due to all the blood spattered on it) and a couple of pilfered rifles slung across his back. Jacobson set the backpack down next to Dane then tossed me a rifle and a moderate supply of ammo. Mimicking Jacobson, I slung the rifle over my shoulder before stowing the ammo in my backpack. Dane and Jacobson had a quick whispered conversation that gave me no small amount of distress.

"Dane you can't!"

Dane walked over and placed his hands on my shoulders. "Miss Pippa. They think I am the Wordsmith. There are numerous ways I can make them think you died with Trevino and give you the chance to get away. You have to make it out of here. I won't even let one thought cross my mind about what could become of you if you don't."

"But, I can't go without you Dane."

'You can if I need you to. It's how I've trained you. Miss Pippa you are one of the most powerful Wordsmiths to have come along in a long time. You will be powerful enough to sit at the head of the Faerie Kin Council as the Hawthorn Wordsmith. I fully believe that. This world is changing; the Council is changing but we both know not for the better. You have the power to set many things right."

"That doesn't explain why you can't come with me. Or why I can't stay. Without me you won't have

I wouldn't say I was taken off guard as much as I was impressed. I had started to think you were some spoiled princess (Pippa Pollywog!) & you were showing some major skill. A woman who can handle herself in that kind of situation is worth respecting.

Having your 61 respect is great gift and compliment

the Words of Power."

"You are the hope I see for the future Pippa. Everything I do, is so that you can bring that hope to the world. Now I need you to go with this young man here and make it home safe."

Barron seemed just as surprised by Dane's words as I was. Dane directed his gaze toward Barron. "Miss Pippa trusts you and so do I. I need you to take her to a temple on the Chinese side of the border where you will find safe transport home. <u>Son, it is likely no one will leave Gehenna alive. I understand you have a wife and you are expecting your first child.</u>"

Barron processed Dane's words beyond coming to comprehend their literal meaning. It took him a moment or two to make his decision. "I will do as you ask."

Jacobson tossed the backpack he'd brought with him to Barron along with the second rifle. As Jacobson gave Barron a quick rundown of the items in the backpack along with the temple coordinates, Dane returned his gaze to me. Many words flew through his mind, but in the end he just hugged me and whispered, "I love you my Princess Pippa Pollywog."

When Dane released me he turned once more to Barron, tossing him a familiar black drawstring bag. "Trust Miss Pippa. She is strong and powerful. You'll know when to use those".

With that Dane and Jacobson disappeared into the shadows and I was left staring forlornly at Barron who gestured in the direction of the origin of the faint breeze I had felt earlier. "We are going through there. I will guard from the rear."

62

Now there was a man who could communicate more in a single look than a textbook. Somehow he knew Gehenna was going to be razed. That much I got. He was guaranteeing my life so long as I could get you out safely.

We labored up the steep incline of the tunnel to the outside in silence. The poor lighting made it difficult for me to see my surroundings, so my mind was too occupied with keeping my feet over the uneven terrain to pay attention to Barron. Even after we ventured into the blinding daylight, slowly picking our way from shadow to shadow, not a word was said between us.

All I can clearly recall from those never ending hours till nightfall of that first day was misery. I had been completely miserable and the weight of it hobbled my movements in an already stressful journey. Every sighing of the wind or rustle of wildlife caused us to jump and look about for pursuers. None ever came, but we still pushed on long after nightfall, pressing to gain what advantage we could.

When I thought I was going to collapse from exhaustion Barron found us a deep cavern to hole up in for the night. Since the cavern was so deep and had such a tall ceiling we hunted about for things to burn in an attempt to ward off the night chill of the Hindu Kush.

As we settled in around our small fire, Barron tossed me an MRE from his backpack. "You have to eat."

Gazing at the dancing flames of the fire I ate my food obediently if absentmindedly. I felt the food renewing me somewhat, but it had only given me more energy with which to be miserable as we sat in silence.

Barron was as exhausted as I was and the food did him the same good as me; only he turned his energy to generating an unending number of unspoken questions that bit at me like a swarm of mosquitoes until he settled on one to ask out loud.

"So what is a Wordsmith?"

"We have the power to sense the auras of words and understand how they affect the human soul."

"So you are mind readers? I am going to be honest I don't much think I believe that to be possible."

"We can't spy on thoughts, but the language of thoughts give off auras; we've honed the ability to interpolate and extrapolate those auras into useful information fairly well. Let me guess, you want me to prove it to you."

"We've got nothing else to do, and I want to know just what I am risking my career and life for here."

"Your career is safe. You have the word of a Wordsmith on that. And if you must have proof then . . . well . . . you were with me from the moment we arrived at Gehenna. You know every word that was spoken to me. But there were ever so many words not spoken out loud. For starters, Gehenna got its name for what it had been- a Taliban prison for torturing U.S. and allied soldiers. The auras in that place made me sick because I sensed the echos of auras that had compounded over a decade or more. You were part of the liberation force that took Gehenna to free the prisoners there six months ago. Your mental language as you recalled your memories during my tour reminded me of the time I talked to a man who had helped liberate Auschwitz."

I paused not sure I wanted to continue, but knowing that Barron needed solid proof.

"I know why everyone was so nervous about my being there; why they felt it was no place for a woman. Since taking over Gehenna, the tables had turned and the captured Taliban members are being tortured for answers. Now before you get upset, subjectively, I understand the hatred that stripped the current prisoners of Gehenna of their humanity in the eyes of their captors. I empathize and even sympathize with the use of the angry, violent, hateful, language that unleashed such explosive and corrosive auras. Objectively, it was hard not to see that the new rulers of Gehenna were mirroring the old; it was hard to reconcile the effects of the blight of war on the souls of good men."

Barron's expression was incredulous and his mental conversation was miffed as his thought language turned to icicle daggers.

"Most of that could have been explained in a briefing before you landed. As for your self-righteous speech you spoiled, overly sheltered, naive, princess, there's no way you could know or understand what we found or how we felt. Do you really know how important it is that we get the answers we are looking for? Do you know what is at stake?"

Searching his mind, I looked for a way to make him see that I had understood. His thoughts made it clear that I was facing a mile high climb up a sheer rock face, only to have to crack an impenetrable fortress at the top. However the auras behind those walls were too strong to be hidden. There was plenty to choose from but only one thing I could come

65

I didn't mean any disrespect to you or your fellow military brethren. I was just trying to process that ordeal

I've gotten used to your speeches by now. But as I am always saying, sometimes less is more when you are trying to make an ally. Especially when dealing with a man's moral compass. What was that George Orwell line, sleeping safe because of rough men that stand ready to visit violence on any who would do us harm?

up with that I felt would be convincing and it was a rather painful memory.

As a Wordsmith I was taught that I was responsible for the potential energy of what I gleaned from someone's mind and the consequences if I should ever release the potential of that information. I hesitated, holding the chosen memory in my mind's eye as it writhed with the potential to turn Barron's rock cliff and fortress to dust.

"You are hunting down a man who has turned the Taliban on its ear from the inside out- whose intentions point to something far worse than any terrorist attack to date. Something you fear will collapse the free world. But I can see that you think I could have been briefed about that as well. So, I am sorry in advance, I don't wish to be cruel, but I need you to believe me. How would I have known that you volunteered to go to Gehenna because you had good reason to believe that your brother-in-law and best friend since kindergarten had been taken there? Or that his family has been informed of his death, but you could never tell your wife or his family about the mutilated state in which you found his body because just thinking about it makes you sick?"

<u>Every word I spoke lashed against Barron's soul, causing it great pain. I hated doing it.</u>

"Just what kind of witch are you?"

It was my turn to flinch against his words.

"What you don't like being called a witch?"

"Do you have any idea what kind of aura that word has? It is full of a venom comprised of fear, hatred, and prejudice."

66

Going to be honest. Your words were validated in your body language, expression, and especially your eyes. I knew by watching you, you weren't lying about understanding me. I couldn't deny a huge reality shift that was staring me in the face. I'll admit it spooked me.

Barron seethed a few moments more and I did what I could to shield myself from the bombardment of auras exploding in his mind. Slowly his mind grew as quiet as the cavern in which we sat, but I could sense his struggle to accept the evidence with which he had been confronted.

"I don't think I fully understand this aura thing."

"I suppose I could clarify. A Wordsmith experiences words in a far more tangible and real way than others. Words to us have smells, sounds, colors, sensations. They also have power. We often categorize them into types using the terms peaceful, enjoyable, healing, harming, explosive, or corrosive auras. We use those terminologies because that is the type of affect we see those words having on the souls that either think, speak, or write them or those toward whom they are being said, thought, or written. We know how to make words heighten or negate the auras of people's souls"

Barron sat looking into the flames trying to digest my words. "I can't say as I understand a word you are
saying, but I am starting to see why someone would want to capture you. I knew a beautiful woman coming to Gehenna was bad news."

I couldn't help but blush at Barron's referring to me as beautiful. "The original Wordsmith was to be a man."

"You mean you aren't the only Wordsmith? How many are there?"

"Not that many compared to the population of the world, but several. Somehow I was the only they could call in and I am not even due to officially start as a Wordsmith till next month."

"The expert is suddenly pulled and a 'not even a rookie yet' is sent into a situation that turns out like this? Smells fishy to me."

Barron's agitation grew and the auras of his mind made me skittish. I had the sensation of a rider who knows there is no way out other than to coerce his horse to cross the pit of vipers they are facing; or maybe I felt more like the horse, wanting to rear and run away. But, I knew I couldn't.

"Dane thought so too."

"The Booker guy, his name was really Dane, huh? So what's yours? Pippen? Pippy?"

"Pippa. Pippa Hawthorn."

"Alright Pippa, since you think you can read minds I should go ahead and tell you that I am not overly fond of running off like this. Your man Dane was suspiciously prepared for our escape. I left good men behind back there with him and the more I get out of you the less comfortable I am with that part of my decision."

"Dane always over prepares . . . Wait you think that he planned that whole thing back there? To what end?"

"Black ops are more dangerous because of those who order them; they tend to send in specialists. For all I know you were there to stop up a leak or something and then your man was to cleanse the place as it were."

"Dane would never do such a thing! I've known him most of my life and he has never been that sort of person."

"How could you know that, your mind reading

trick? I'm still having a hard time believing that line. That Dane guy had the look of black ops and wet works all over him. <u>I seriously doubt he's the righteous guardian angel you think him to be.</u>"

I had grown desperate to clear Dane's name. Odd. Looking back I didn't have any care whatsoever what Barron thought of me. I just couldn't stand the thought that anyone could think of Dane as such a
villain. I know the man wasn't a saint, but. . .

"What can I do to prove to you I am a Wordsmith?"

"Well, not by telling me things you could have picked up while in Gehenna. How about this- can you tell me about my wife? Like what's her name?"

I let Barron's thoughts wander for a bit so I could piece together a story from the auras. The progression of auras reminded me of the auras described by the Master Wordsmith C.S. Lewis as the Natural Loves.

Affection: being a familiarity or a peaceful and joyous stability; with the warmth of sunshine and the smell of fresh air and the sounds of carefree laughter.

Phillas, brotherly love and the love of friendship, indicative of being intrinsically understood by someone; the deep trust and sense of adventure and camaraderie of facing a challenge together.

The auras wandered into the passionate heat, magnetism, and pleasure of Eros; I didn't linger too long in those thoughts.

Watching Barron as he recalled his wife and home the words of another Master Wordsmith,

You have lived up 69 to it Barron, in ever so many ways.

See previous notes- this old guy obviously knew more than he was telling you, but you were too trusting to question him. Now that you've given me that same trust I understand how it can make men desperate to live up to it.

J.R.R. Tolkien, popped to mine. It was a quote from one of my favorite characters, Faramir, and in watching Barron and attending to the auras in his thoughts it took on new life.

"I do not love the bright sword for its sharpness, nor the arrow for its swiftness, nor the warrior for his glory. I love only that which they defend."

I was deeply moved by what I sensed in Barron. I did not know if I could get him to trust and respect me, but in that moment I completely trusted and respected him. I took a deep breath and shook myself from the warmth and comfort of the auras in Barron's thoughts.

"Wordsmiths can't discern names. When someone thinks of their name or the names of others, all their thoughts and feelings for that person surface. Names are powerful, they sum up the entirety of a person. It is a blessing we can't discern names. But I do know, you've known her your whole life. You first proposed when you were in the . . . the third grade, I think. She wouldn't agree to marry you till after she'd finished her masters in counseling. You've been married for five years. You had a month of leave nine months ago for a second honeymoon and well . . ."

I fiercely hoped that the red in my cheeks was being construed as being flushed because of the fire. I couldn't stop myself from quickly rushing through my conclusion.

". . . it was very enjoyable. And now you are expecting your first child any day, which is why they

70

Oh, I noticed. It was something watching you turn every shade of red. Still makes me laugh.

But back then I laughed partly from relief. You weren't normal, but you were at least sincere.

True, I'm not normal, but if I was your life would be so much more boring Fair enough.

are letting you go home for a few days before they give you your reassignment from Gehenna."

Barron's laughter filled the cave for several minutes during which my discomfort only grew.

"Okay, I can't say I get what it means to be a Wordsmith, but I get that what you do would be helpful with what we were doing in Gehenna and is something I don't want any enemy to get their hands on. And sorry for that last bit, I truly hadn't meant to embarrass you. Though, you seemed to handle the men in the canteen fairly well. I know what kind of thoughts were flying around in there, them having seen their first flesh and blood woman in so long- not to mention one as attractive as you."

"You are awfully free with your compliments for a married man who is well . . . from what I can tell very, very happily married."

It was Barron's turn to blush slightly. "My wife knows I'm not blind. And she's the one who tells me to compliment women when one crosses my mind; because 'most women don't hear honest compliments often enough'. She's a counselor for troubled youth. According to her, 'no one hears compliments often enough and the human soul needs to hear words of compliments and encouragement to be healthy and strong'. She often says the kids she works with would have a better time of it if someone had spoken more kindly to them on a consistent basis. Come to think of it, you two would get on like best friends."

"She sounds like someone I'd love to meet."

"We should probably think about sleep. You familiar with watches?"

"<u>They are small time keeping devices worn on the wrist. The word watch has roots from c.1200 meaning 'the division of night into periods of time'; translating from Latin *vigilia*, Greek *phylake*, and the Hebrew</u>

ashmoreth. <u>Used as military term for 'guard or sentinel' circa the 14th century.</u>"

"I am going to take that as a yes. I'll take the first watch."

Every day after followed a similar pattern. During the day we covered as much ground as possible and every night around the fire we kept conversing to come to understand one another. <u>There were plenty of close calls and hair raising moments in our 16 day journey, but the one that distinguishes itself from the rest began late on our 14th day of travel.</u>

It had been two days since I had even sensed the aura of another human's mind other than Barron's. We'd stopped alongside a glacial stream to refill our water when I felt the first twinges of strong auras. By that time Barron and I had formed a strong bond. He seemed to have sharper instincts than most people and could guess my mind before I could even fully

register the truth of a situation. It was a trait that painfully reminded me of Dane.

"What are you sensing?"

"Several men. Moving too fast to be on foot. A bit more than a mile out."

"We talking like on donkeys, elephants, unicycles, or what?"

The minds were too far away to get a clear read on all the auras but one or two stood out enough for me to hazard a guess. "Dirt bikes?"

"So no out running them. I don't like the idea of just hunkering down either. Let's see if we can skirt them where they won't be able to easily travel on those bikes. Maybe we'll get lucky and they aren't even looking for us. If we play it right maybe we can get us a ride to the Chinese border."

And that's what we did, we skulked along the high jagged rock ridges where no bike could reach. Judging by the dirt bikes' wide and double backing patterns of movement our luck wasn't holding out. Those men were definitely searching for something and their dragnet was pulling tighter around us.

That night there was no conversation, no fire, and no sleep. The night fall slowed the movements of the dirt bikes with their searchlight bright lamps, so we made a play for whatever advantage we could get using the cover of darkness. We didn't even pause to eat or drink, just getting down our throats what we could while still on the move. We tried to pace ourselves so that exhaustion wouldn't overtake us before our pursuers did.

However, just before daylight, Barron stopped; ducking into a cave with a highly defensible rock outcrop to its front he declared we had to rest. What he wasn't saying out loud was that he knew we were close to being surrounded and he'd decided that was as good a place as any to lay low and hope that they missed us in the dark.

It felt good to get off my feet, but neither of us

really relaxed as we each kept reorganizing our supplies and ammo. At one point I saw Barron pull out the drawstring bag that Dane had tossed him just before we were left alone. It started me thinking about a few things.

Inside the drawstring bag were noise canceling headphones that Dane carried for when I chose to use Heavenly Words of Power. Yes, we tell people Words of Power are the right words to achieve the desired results in a given situation, but there were also Heavenly Words of Power that only a Wordsmith knows or can use. There is no language in the Twin Worlds of the World of Men or in the World of Faerie that a Wordsmith cannot master. But the Heavenly languages are all but a mystery to even us. All powerful and commanding, the Heavenly languages can alter the reality of everything under Heaven, in both the World of Men and the World of Faerie. Since the time the Wordsmiths came into being in this world, they have encountered and mastered a hand full of words belonging to the Heavenly languages.

At that time I had only just mastered one of the Heavenly Words of Power. It was what we Wordsmiths refer to as Babel; being that which was spoken over the Tower of Babel sending the world's languages into chaos. Babel is one of the first Heavenly Words of Power a Wordsmith is taught. Most Wordsmiths can attain enough mastery over Babel to use it in thought to confuse and stun people around them (yes it has power even in mere thought and even then we only use a few syllables of the whole), but it can take decades to master Babel to the point it can be used verbally. Using Babel can do irreversible damage to the one who uses it and to those on whom it is used.

Speaking Heavenly Words of Power out loud is taboo for all but a Master Wordsmith. At Dane's insistence that I was capable of achieving Master Wordsmith standing before even officially taking the oaths of a Wordsmith, I had been working to master Babel. If only I had been working on Lazarus (a Heavenly Word of Power to summon a soul from the afterlife) as well, then Trevino. . .

Waiting until Barron was lightly dozing, I pulled the drawstring bag out of his things and put it on my belt for easy access.

As the black of night turned charcoal grey, Barron and I ventured out with a mind to steal a couple of dirt bikes and make a run for it. Having doubled checked our coordinates against our destination, there was a slim chance we could make it.

Our teamwork was impeccable. We'd been tracking the search patterns of the men on dirt bikes and had determined when certain men in the pattern would be the most isolated from the rest. It was a matter of distracting and disposing of the dirt bikes' riders before we were zipping through the Hindu Kush on our newly acquired vehicles.

Our plan had been going well, which meant we were due for things to go wrong. First our disregard for maintaining the pattern in favor of simply attempting to make a straight run for our destination garnered more attention that we could have anticipated.

By then you'd become a pretty good partner. I was sort of getting used to your little advantages in a fight. Still I had no idea what kind of advantages you really have.

75

Second, one of the dirt bikes had managed to obtain a leak in its fuel line and my dirt bike started to sputter out. Before we even had the chance to have a proper argument about my taking the working dirt bike we were surrounded.

I didn't even give it a second thought, I just pulled the drawstring bag from my belt and shoved it into Barron's hands. "Put these on and don't ask questions."

"I wondered why you stole those out of my stuff. Is this the part where I get to see the all-powerful Wordsmith at work?"

"I said no questions, be sure to power those things on. You have got to trust me. Oh, and recite something to yourself. Think about your wife, your baby."

Barron gave a slight nod and put on the headphones. When I saw the little green light I knew it was safe to go to work. But I sensed Barron's mind was still focused on the situation at hand. I gave him a sharp look. Begrudgingly, he turned his thoughts to other things. When I heard him mentally reciting his marriage vows, I felt his mind was safeguarded enough to proceed.

It takes an incredible amount of concentration to use Heavenly Words of Power and I had not had any training that came close to preparing me for the situation in which we had found ourselves. My senses were painfully acute and not even the tiniest aura or physical sensation was lost on me. That is how I came to feel the slight itching of the chain around my neck from the necklace Dane had given me for my 18th birthday a few years before. Dane

Can't blame a man for being curious. Not to mention zoning out in the middle of a battle went against the grain something fierce.

believed in me and in all my years with him he had never given me a reason to doubt him. It was time for me to believe in myself as Dane did. I took a deep cleansing breath before reciting a chant to neutralize all the auras that could influence me before reciting Babel.

Heavenly Words of Power are far longer than words are understood to be on Earth and each syllable holds its own unique power. For Babel to be effective each syllable has to be given the proper emphasis in combination with those around it. As I projected Babel aloud everything under the sound of my voice slowed until they became frozen in a split second outside of time. With at great roll of thunder Babel was completed and everything was released back into time in total chaos.

The men who had been pursuing us looked at one another as they would total strangers. There was an aura of total fear about the men in the wake of Babel as they began to regard one another as threats to be eliminated. Before our eyes our pursuers wiped themselves out.

<u>I'll never forget the look of horror on Barron's face and I'll never be able to assuage the sting of his thoughts directed toward me in that moment. To be honest his thoughts echoed my own.</u> I knew Babel was dangerous, but I had no idea just what to expect from using it aloud. I thought it just caused confusion. I couldn't help but wonder if I had messed up some part of the Heavenly Word to cause this tragedy. And I could only hope my own expression conveyed my own shock.

When the mountainside grew quiet I turned

I still feel bad about this. I'll never forget the look on your face, Pippa. I haven't forgotten what went through my mind. You should never have heard those words, no one ever should. By that time I knew what a tough but kind & caring person you are, still I let my shock get the better of me

I didn't realize it till it was too late & I was certain you'd do yourself harm.

77

from Barron and started to run. I really hadn't had a destination in my mind, I just couldn't be near Barron and his thoughts a second longer. Unheeding of my path I ran with the world turning into a kaleidoscope from my tears. It is a wonder I hadn't tripped sooner. My hands planted in something warm and sticky and the smell of urine and bowel movements accosted my senses. Looking, down I saw that I had slipped in a puddle of blood that had collected from two of our pursuers. I threw up and couldn't stop shaking; wracking sobs stole my ability to breath.

<u>Barron trotted up and tried to put his arms around me to calm me down but I fought them off. I was angry. At Barron. At Dane. At myself.</u>

"Get away from me!"

"Pippa, what on earth? Why are you fighting me?"

"Stay away from me, Barron. I'm a monster. You think so too!"

"Pippa, I was surprised, who wouldn't be? But clearly you were even more surprised than me."

Barron took a step toward me, and I scrambled away from him; barely avoiding tripping over corpses.

"Pippa, you are powerful, but you are no monster. A monster wouldn't have this kind of reaction; a human does. And not just a human, but a human I would trust and value as a friend. Let me help you Pippa."

As he spoke he slowly progressed toward me. I wanted to keep pushing him away, but the world became fuzzy. I held my head and fought to maintain my balance.

She makes it sound like a toddler flailing their arms. No. She pulled out her best Bruce Lee impersonation. And she was serious about it. If I'd had less than first class military training she'd have broken all my bones!

Since when are you given to exaggeration? 78 Since never! I've got scars where you clawed my arm!

"Pippa, what's going on? Are you okay?"

I dropped to the ground and sat in a sprawled position holding my head in my hands. I heard Barron's footsteps and felt him next to me before the world disappeared into a black nothingness.

I awoke surrounded by a flurry of new auras. The feeling jolted me up right and onto my feet, but the exertion made me woozy and I nearly collapsed back to the floor of the cave in which I found myself. I was swept up into Barron's arms and he settled me back on a stack of reed mats where I had been lying.

"Easy Pippa. These guys are from the temple that Dane wanted us to reach. They came to meet us. This is Head Monk, Wei Chen."

"It is most fortunate for us that we did not arrive sooner or else we too might have succumb to Babel. It can manifest in many ways for, you see, no one outside of Heaven are meant to speak the Words of Heaven. For you it manifested violently."

I turned to look at the man who was speaking, he was dressed as a monk of the Shaolin order. All around were other monks milling about working to get food prepared; each was dressed in monochromatic robes of orange, red, yellow, green, blue, or brown. It was the first time in my life that I was able to identify someone as a Faerie Kin by simply looking at them. I didn't know how or why, but I knew that every monk in the cave with us was a Faerie Kin.

"I see you have the sight now."

I didn't know what to do other than I had to protect you. Or die a moment before you. 79 That was most likely.
They went from fierce warriors to mild monks when they saw I was protecting you To think that's the least weird experience I've had

It was quite the show when those monk showed up. You'd just cast a Tolkien level spell then collapsed on the bloodiest battlefield I've ever seen. Then suddenly I was out of Middle Earth é in a Kung Fo flick. All these monks popped out of thin air é were flying about in impossible acrobatics

I returned my gaze to the head monk. "What?"

"Don't strain yourself. Using the Words of Heaven take a toll on the soul. It is a testament to your strength and heart that you even made it through Babel at your age, let alone managed to remain conscious for as long as you did afterward. By using the Words of Heaven you have become aware of the part of your soul that is destined to reside there and you can now see things that you could not before."

"You mean she's more powerful now than she was?"

<u>Looking at Barron I was shocked to see that he too was a Faerie Kin; though somehow it was clear that he had no idea of his lineage.</u>

"Hmm. One is born with the power of the universe, but we can each only become aware of that power in small portions at a time. I would say Miss Pippa has simply become more aware of a larger portion of the power of the universe in a single moment than most people have in their lifetimes. Dane was correct in his assessment of this child."

"Dane! He stayed behind in Gehenna!"

"Be calm, dear child. I see that you have not gained the knowledge of patience and peace from the universe. We have sent monks to search for him and give him aid should they find him. You must rest. We will set out for the temple tomorrow and then find a way to get you in touch with the Faerie Kin Council. No doubt they will be anxious to hear of how you fare."

There was an aura around the Head Monk as he spoke of the Faerie Kin Council that made me uneasy. It was clear he did not trust the Council and

A fact you never bothered to tell me.

I didn't think it mattered at the time.
Wait who told you?

that he was loath to have any contact with them. That aside, there was nothing about the monks that gave me any reason to doubt them.

><*

Two days later we were in a Wordsmith estate just outside of Bangkok, Thailand. Barron's parents had been flown out to meet him. We both thought it a little odd, but nothing could prepare us for why they had come. Barron's wife had been in a car accident. She managed to survive long enough to give birth. The child however was also weakened from the accident and only lived just under 36 hours after birth.

All the anguish of Gehenna could not match that which flooded Barron's soul in the wake of the news. I had not been present when he had heard the news; indeed I heard the news from the shrieks of Barron's mind that brought me to my knees in the middle of the garden path I was walking to go and see him. I had wanted to tell him my own parents had come. I couldn't bring myself to go see Barron after that. It was my fault he hadn't been there. I know it is irrational to say that I in any way affected the car accident; but if Barron hadn't been with me he would have at least gotten to say goodbye to his wife and hold his son at least once.

Had it not been for our parents bringing us together for an evening meal prior to the morning of Barron's departure, I would not have been able to face him. Neither of us ate anything. We spent the meal looking at anything but another human. In the end as we were making our way from the dining

81

And apparently you hadn't been paying attention. Someone meant to kill you; I would have been nothing more than collateral damage if I hadn't gone with you. Who or why, I am still trying to figure out — trust me, I will room we simultaneously turned to one another.

"Barron, I am so sorry! I wish . . . if only I had . . . if I could . . ."

"Pippa. . . I . . ."

"Thank you. You saved my life. I am forever in your debt . . . and yet you've lost. . ."

Barron pulled me into a hug. I could feel the warmth and wet of tears in my hair. I too was crying into Barron's shoulder. We stood there like that for several minutes before Barron whispered. "Thank you Pippa."

Letting go, Barron walked down the hall away from me and didn't even turn around when I called out, "For what?"

And that was how I spent my vacation summer before last. I've been thinking about that time a lot lately. I think it is because I am being hounded to choose a security detail. I just can't bring myself to do it. They sent a Hawthorn Private Security Force team to sweep Gehenna in hopes of finding Dane, but they tell me that the place was burned out and no recognizable human remains were to be found. For all I know Dane and Jacobson are dead. Without those men, there really isn't anyone I want for my security detail except one.

I went to see Barron in Hawaii in the last few days
before his discharge but I couldn't bring myself
to actually approach him. I just don't know what I would say.

I've been on any number of missions since Gehenna and was officially named the youngest Master Wordsmith in recent history. And now, here I sit, posing as a substitute teacher proctoring 'how I spent my summer vacation' essays while attempting to ferret out an underage accomplice for a sex trafficking ring in a preppy high school in California. The target is not a sophomore, thus the reason I am writing this to keep boredom at bay. Though possibly I just need to give some order to my thoughts.

I got the word last week that I am to be the Hawthorn in residence at Hawthorn Heights. I should make sure to pack my sweaters for a New England fall.

I still can't believe you went all the way to Hawaii and didn't think I'd want to see you. The truth is that I had been thinking about our time in the Hindu Kush as well. Actually, more about Bangkok.

I know you know, but I was a mess after I lost Liza and my son, Liam. I was reassigned to Hawaii & everyone gave me a wide berth for a while. But every time someone would try to get me to talk about it, or my feelings. Every time they'd try to say they understood, I just got so mad, because I knew they didn't. No one understood the kind of pain I was going through. But every time I'd think that, the memory of you hitting the garden walk in Bangkok would flash through my mind.

I saw you that day & I knew you felt everything I did. You felt you needed to appologize but you didn't pity me because you nderstood. You didn't hold my feelings against me. That stuck with me. You became the only person in the world who could understand, who could help me. Because believe me, I knew I needed help.

I found a business card in that bag with the headphones. It was Dane Ford's for the Hawthorn Private Security Force. I hadn't been home a week after my discharge before I knew I couldn't stay in my hometown. I stuck it out for a month but that card was in my hands every five minutes or so.

I finally decided to call. They were so happy that I did. Not only did they remember me, they were hoping I would call. Apparently you were refusing to name a security detail & had taken to ditching whatever one's they'd assign to you. Did you know your parents met me at the headquarters? They told me about you visiting Hawaii & they begged me to please

take the job- the only hitch was you'd
have to agree.

So I take the job & they dispatch me to
California where I found you trying to
take down a sex trafficing ring all by
your self. I still get mad thining about it.

We've never really talked about it, but
like I said before, I never blamed you
for Liza and Liam. If anything you were
the only one I could turn to after I lost
them. We've been working together for 5 &
a half years (doing some hair raising jobs
that I still have a hard time believing
were real) & I can say that meeting you
saved my life more than once.

You taught me to live again. You saw the
good volunteering at the rec center did for
me. How it made me feel like I was
continuing Liza's work & you pushed me to
pursue it & even made it possible to be

the director.

You've always supported me 100%. With you by my side I felt that I had a life to live. One where I could laugh. One where I could do some good & accept good things offered to me. One where I could love agian.

Wow.

I should probably tell you all this in person.

Well it is about time one of you did! Squee! I am just so excited! I am jumping about like a fool and I think I just gave Chaucer a heart attack by picking him up and swinging him around.

Of Wordsmiths & Faerie Kin & Sealing Spells & Dreams

Excerpts from the private journal of Constance Peters

For Constance,

May you always write your life in your own words. Just be sure to choose them wisely!

Affectionately Yours,

Pippa Hawthorn & Barron

August 25

As of today I start my life as a university student, I figure it is as good a time as any to start recording my journey in the journal given to me by Barron and Pippa. This has to be the most beautiful journal I've ever seen. The exquisite hawthorn trees tooled on the covers had to be done by a master leather craftsman; and I am fairly sure the gold gilding is real. As are the gold clasp lock and the key that is set with precious stones. I wear the key around my neck on a gold chain.

Pippa & Barron left Hawthorn Heights the 1st of June and I haven't heard from them since. I also haven't heard from this new Hawthorn Wordsmith coming into town. Not that he has to come introduce himself, but I am living in the Carriage House on Hawthorn Ringed Land; being among a precious few true sanctuaries for Wordsmiths and Faerie Kin on earth. I guess I just thought he'd stop by.

Goodness! I thought I had more time! I'll have to finish this later!

I probably shouldn't be carrying this journal around, but I just couldn't stop myself from throwing it into my bag when I ran out of the Carriage House today. I suppose it is for the best, at least this way I can get my newest most embarrassing moment recorded while it is fresh in my mind.

So I had taken longer to do my chores, pick out

an outfit, and get dressed than I thought. The plan had been to have a nice cup of tea and record my thoughts about going to university today, but that obviously didn't happen.

Pippa left me her Range Rover for use while she's gone, but that thing is ancient and of course it chose to act out this morning; which put me even later than I was already. Then I couldn't find my lecture hall. Now I blame Hawthorn University for that one. Hawthorn University is one of the oldest universities in the country. It sits on the east end of Hawthorn Park. I do love its variety of architecture, but it seems that they haven't come up with a standardized way of numbering their classrooms yet. Apparently they just use the next number in line, no matter if the two rooms with neighboring numbers are in buildings across campus from one another.

All that tempting of writer's cramp to say that I was late for my first class. I slipped into my Introduction to Humanities class as quietly as I could. I'd only missed the opening remarks. It was clear the professor was annoyed with me, but thankfully he didn't call me out. This guy I could only guess was the TA (I missed the introductions) brought me a syllabus.

My instinct was to avoid eye contact and just get the syllabus from him. But I was caught off guard by his scent. I can't believe I just wrote that. It wasn't that choking, eye burning, kind of scent from someone with too much aftershave or cologne. It was a subtle, but enveloping, somehow familiar kind of scent. Add the fact that he held the paper so that I had to look at him to retrieve it, I couldn't help but look him straight in his sparkling blue-brown topaz eyes. As a heat began to rise into my cheeks I quickly snatched the paper away from the guy and turned my head downward to fish something out of my bag before he could notice me blushing.

Oh, for goodness sake, I sound like a teen romance novel. What happened next won't help save me from such a fate either. As I was pulling out a pen and a notebook, I was so flustered I managed to spill the contents of my bag and they bounced and scattered all the way down the steps to the front of the room.

Everyone turned to look at me and I froze; turning every shade of red with my heart beating out of my chest. The curvy girl with beach waved hair wearing a pale sage peasant shirt and flower print boho skirt who occupied the seat in front of mine and the TA helped me pick my things up while the professor stood silently brooding waiting for us to finish.

The TA seemed amused by the whole situation. In fact long after everyone else had finally stopped staring at me, I would catch him looking my direction. Every time my face would flush anew which would make him chuckle.

That smirk of his! Handsome and charming are two adjectives anyone would use for the guy, but there was something under the surface that comes out in that smirk. It is something that makes me think he'd be cast as the somewhat less than scrupulous rival to a movie's heartthrob hero.

It annoys me how often I tried to sneak a look at

him only to get caught. I'm going to chalk it up to a sense of gratitude for having aided me. I wanted to thank him. That's all. But, He ducked out of the lecture hall after class too quickly for me to even think of approaching him to thank him for his help.

I did get to thank the girl in front of me. Her name is Vidette Salbei. If I had to summarize her in one word it would be Genuine. I think she is going to be fun to get to know. I am actually waiting on her to go to lunch together as I write this.

The rest of my day went smoothly and I even managed to make a new friend, as well as catch up with old ones from high school. I guess I should say that the rest of my day went smoothly until I got home to the Carriage House; which was rather late as I had dinner with my dad and sisters.

The first thing I noticed were scattered lights on in the Carriage House, but that didn't alarm me too much; I'd run out so quickly and I tend to forget lights anyway. Then when I went in through the laundry room entrance I was met by a frantic Beatrix and Chaucer. Something had greatly upset them.

Being on Hawthorn Ringed Land, not just anyone can find their way to the Carriage House. You have to be shown by a Hawthorn or be Faerie Kin to even see the Hawthorn Tree sentinels that guard the entrance to the Hawthorn Ringed Land. I'd learned from experience that not all Faerie Kin are friendly, but every single one of them has some kind of extraordinary power.

As I pulled a scimitar off its hanging hooks on the wall, I doubted it would do any good against a Faerie Kin, especially if they were Argonauts. God help me if it turned out to be an heir to the Wrath of Achilles or Gilgamesh! Keeping to the shadows I slowly made my way into the main hall. I saw and heard nothing unusual until there was a flash of a shadow across the stone of the fireplace that had to originate from the old loft upstairs. With as much stealth as I could muster I snuck up the turret steps. Creeping from shadow to shadow until I ringed the loft, I finally caught sight of someone with their back to me reading over something setting on the desk.

For the second time that day I froze; I had no idea what to do next. Did I just jump out and wave my sword like a lunatic? Did I sneak up behind them and warn them the cops had been notified? That wouldn't work, the cops don't even know this place exists and they couldn't find it if anyone had asked them to look. I mean I don't think I could really just kill someone, let alone from behind without warning. Seriously though, it is one thing to know something in theory; being faced with the possibility of having to transform theory into practice proved more challenging than I had thought it would be.

I had been so wrapped up in my almost panic I hadn't noticed that the person had disappeared. While I had been trying to decide how to get the drop in them, they had gotten the drop on me. Sensing someone behind me, my muscle memory propelled me out of dormancy and I flew at the intruder. A man. That was the first thing I figured out about the intruder. The second was he was no slouch with the saber he had borrowed from Don Quixote- the upstairs suite of armor made up of all manner of armaments from around the world. I made sure to do a visual sweep over in Don's direction to ascertain if he still had his katana, halberd, and other sharp objects.

I wish I'd the skill to describe the fight, but in all honesty it happened so quickly for me I don't even really know what happened. Other than we managed to range the entirety of the Carriage House in the course of the duel, I also recall some stupendous acrobatics on both of our parts. Then at some point, we lost the swords and I got the upper hand as I have always been better at unarmed combat. I'd just managed to get the guy in a wrist-lock when he called out, "Alright you win! You win!"

I was startled by his deep rich English accent and for the first time took a close look at his face. I loosed my hold in shock when I saw it was the TA from my humanities class. My brain started to spark and things began to fall into place.

"Rhys Hawthorn? Why didn't you say anything?"

"Well, to be honest I kind of wanted to see how good you were. And I'd say you've had some first class training. Not to mention a ferocious fighting spirit." Rhys was rubbing the wrist I'd had in a lock; I hadn't held back and he was lucky I hadn't broken it. "Good on you by the way, learning how

to do all this to take down that blighter who at-
tacked you."

My face was red again, I knew it had to be, but
I wasn't certain if it was from embarrassment or
anger. "I don't mean now, well . . . yes now . . .
but earlier at school."

"I had somewhere to be. And you were late
to class. I saw your name on the roster, but there
were other absent girl's names on the roster that
you could have fit. You know how we Wordsmiths
fair with discerning names, I assume. I'm glad it
was you though. I knew I liked you the moment
you came in the room. You have a very interesting
mind. Of course if you've been tutored by a Wordsmith, and a Hawthorn Wordsmith at that, you'd
have to be special."

My face had been flushed for so much of the
day, if I'd been watching me in third person I'd
have thought I had a fever. If I did have a fever it
went up a few more degrees at Rhys' words. I felt
a gentle pressure on my foot and looked down to
see Beatrix and Chaucer. Beatrix wanted to be held
and I was glad of the distraction as I knelt down
to pet and reassure them both before picking up
Beatrix.

"Not to seem rude, but what are you doing
here Mr. Hawthorn?"

"Rhys, if you please. I flew in late last night
and decided to come by to pay my respects to the
keeper of the Carriage House, but you weren't
here. So I let myself in. I didn't think you'd be so
late getting in, you just don't give off the vibe of a
girl that hangs out late. But I get a family dinner. I
would have left, but I got to looking through some

99

books and lost track of time."

Rhys reached out to pet Beatrix, but she shied away. I also felt Chaucer snuggle in closer to my ankle.

"Those little guys don't much like me, it would seem."

"They don't like uninvited strangers in their house. Well, Chaucer just simply doesn't like strangers."

"I'm sorry to have startled you little ones, but this is technically my house for the time being. My cousin just decided someone else should be its caretaker. Not that I mind, I've too much to do at the university to take care of all these animals. Not to mention that loft is closer. Sorry to ramble on. I can see you are already tired of my presence tonight so I shall make my greetings and leave you. I am Rhys Hawthorn."

Rhys offered me his hand. I shifted Beatrix into the crook of one arm to be able to accept it.

"I am Constance Peters."

To my great surprise he gently caught my fingertips pulled them to his lips.

"I am honored to make your acquaintance Constance Peters. Please forgive my intrusion. I am truly sorry for the unpleasant memories you had to revisit during our duel, but I must say I do know you much better in one meeting than I could have hoped. Since we are linked, you and I, by this place and whatever fate awaits us, I am pleased to find myself in such gracious and splendid company."

He kissed my hand once more as he bowed low.

"I shall take my leave."

I could only stand stunned as I watched him exit through the laundry room.

September 15

I had that strange dream again. I always feel as if I haven't had a wink of sleep when the dream comes to visit. It gets more bizarre every time I have it. It always starts with a voice; an ancient voice so graveled and wheezing with age I can't tell if it is male or female. At first they speak a language I cannot understand, but as the warm glow of fire appears and strengthens to illuminate the scene, so does my understanding of the voice's words. We are always around a fire, but the location is always different. Sometimes we are outdoors and other times indoors; sometimes there are modern trappings and other times it is clear we are in an ancient dwelling; sometimes it is humble and other times it is a palace decadent beyond description.

The speaker is always hidden in the shadows. What I can see of them is wrinkled and sagging. I've caught sight of an ear clearly once and it was huge; weighted down with a gold and emerald drop earing, the lobe drapes over the speaker's shoulder. What I can tell about their clothes is they seem to be a gallimaufry of fabrics swathed and wrapped about them.

The shape of the shadow suggests a turban on their head with wild tufts of hair poking out at odd intervals. The only thing I always see clearly is their hands which are elephantine, a dirty tan brown, and calloused with knuckles greatly knotted with arthritis; adorned with massive rings sparkling from a variety of precious stones. One hand is always on a knee to keep their bowed hunchbacked frame marginally upright; the other hand holding a poker to prod the fire.

The speaker is telling me a story I first heard from Pippa. However this time I am directed to keep an eye on the fire where the flames wreath about until they form pantomime for me to watch. The longer the story carries on, the more colorful and holographic the quality the flame's panto becomes. It is the story of the Hawthorn Tree, the first Faerie Kin.

The world was born as twins; one the World of Faerie, the other the World of Men. The World of Fairies was the elder twin, and it first saw light long before the younger World of Men. As they were being created they knew of one another, but could not communicate to one another until a tree was called forth from both worlds at once, the Hawthorn.

Growing simultaneously on the World of Faerie and the World of Men, the Hawthorn watched over them both; acting as a gatekeeper between the worlds. Being the elder twin, the World of Fairies rejoiced as it had been watching its sibling grow and was eager to visit. The Hawthorn became the most sacred tree in the World of Fairies and they doted on it.

However as inhabitants of the World of Faerie came to the World of Men they quickly realized that they couldn't long survive in the World of Men, for there was no natural magic there. The peoples of the World of Faerie did what they could to teach the inhabitants of the World of Men about magic, but it would seem the younger World of Men had no talent for it. Indeed it did not seem to desire the knowledge of magic for it preferred the knowledge of science. And so magic could only dwell on the World of Men in small spots, usually in the vicinity of a Hawthorn, and it was never strong enough to let a Faerie live very long before having to return to the World of Faerie.

Now trees in the World of Faeries are much more alive than trees in the World of Men for their souls are strong enough to express themselves. A Hawthorn has two souls, one that is strong and active in the World of Fairies and the other that is weak and dormant in the World of Men. In the time when the World of Men could be counted a toddler, the Young Son of a farmer ran away from home most upset. He climbed into the branches of the Hawthorn tree on the family farm and began to talk to the tree of his troubles. As most trees are ignored by Men, the Hawthorn was so surprised by the Boy's earnest confiding that its soul in the World of Men awoke.

As the Boy grew into a man, eventually becoming the Farmer on the family farm, he would always climb up in the branches of the Hawthorn; speaking to it of his troubles and his joys. With every visit, the soul of the Hawthorn in the World of Men grew stronger until it surpassed the strength of its soul in the World of Faerie.

The Hawthorn shared all of life's joys and hardships with the Farmer. As a young man, the Farmer would secretly meet his love under the Hawthorn and it was there he took the woman to be his wife. When the Farmer and his wife had children, they would bring them to have picnics and play beneath and in the branches of the Hawthorn. The Hawthorn, in turn would invite Fairies to come play, though it seemed that the Farmer and his wife could not see the Fairies. Eventually the children could no longer see them either, and seemed to forget that they existed. But each of them fell in love with the Hawthorn; always remembering it to be a magical place. The Hawthorn watched the children of the Farmer grow up and fall in love and in turn bring their children to play beneath its adoring shelter.

The Hawthorn wept with the Farmer when he lost loved ones, when fire destroyed his home, when he had to bury his sons lost in war and his daughter and grandson to childbirth. But then came the day that the Farmer died and was buried beneath the Hawthorn's watch. The Hawthorn had been broken hearted when the Farmer suffered in life, but life without the Farmer nearly destroyed the Hawthorn. The Faerie were dismayed to find the Hawthorn so sick and close to death. They asked the Hawthorn what they could do to make it happy again. The Hawthorn said it wanted to become human and become a part of the Farmer's family.

The Faerie decided to go to the Father of the Twin Worlds and ask for him to grant the Hawthorn's request. The Father of the Twin Worlds granted the Hawthorn's request, but warned that it would change both worlds. Faerie would be able to more freely move about in the World of Men and humans would have easier access to the World of Faerie. The Human Hawthorn and his descendants would be responsible for keeping balance and order between the two worlds in the World of Men.

The Hawthorn became the first Faerie Kin, the first child of both Twin Worlds. He arrived in human form the day the family had gathered to mourn the loss of the Hawthorn tree and something about the stranger comforted them. They invited him into their home, hiring him to help around the farm, and eventually the Hawthorn married the Farmer's youngest granddaughter.

As it was Words that worked magic to awaken the Hawthorn's soul in the World of Men, he and his descendants had power over words unlike other men. They became the Wordsmiths.

A quick prod from the fire poker and the flames spark and settle into their usual rhythmic undulations. Having been so entranced by the flames, their spell suddenly being undone nearly almost always leaves me a breath away from falling into their fiery embrace. It is in that moment that I first get the sensation that I am but a guest in the mind of another, for my body doesn't respond as I desire.

Then comes the question. Always only one question and my answer is never correct. Granted my answer is seldom ever my own and though the voice that speaks for me is familiar, I cannot recognize it.

Once it was:

"So what are the Wordsmith's?"

"They are the offspring of the Hawthorn."

"No, no you simple girl! Use that brain of yours! They are the guardians of the Fairy Kin, not their dictators."

And another time it was:

"What significance has the Hawthorn Line?"

"The Hawthorn was the first Faerie Kin?"

"Have you not been listening? Without a direct descendant, a Hawthorn Wordsmith, the line of the First Faerie Kin will be lost and all Faerie Kin can no longer live in the World of Men nor can they live in the World of Faerie!"

October 17

It has been nearly two months since I first met
Rhys and I have yet to understand my own mind
as to him. For one thing, even though he is a grad-
uate student TA, he's only two years older than me
(Wordsmith's tend to be brilliant apparently), he
can seem decades older at times and then young
and rash in the next breath. It didn't take him
long to land a lead guitar gig with a popular local
indie band, Elysian, and he is just as natural in his
rock grunge as he is in his ties and slacks as a TA.

He is at once polite and discourteous. I find
him in the Carriage House without warning often,
and though his words of apology for inconve-
niencing me are sincere, they are not apologetic
for committing the act of barging into my home.
He has an annoying habit of goading and compli-
menting me in the same breath.

Rhys Hawthorn may well be devastatingly
handsome with a dashing smile that makes my
heart skip a beat, but I just can't bring myself
to trust him. I guess my doubts started with the
quips about Pippa's having left me in charge of the
Carriage House. Then there were the animals. Beatrix and Chaucer are either in my lap or under my
feet when he is around. The one time he expressed
a desire to ride, I had to let him right Aragorn for
Raijin, Nerida, and Matilda would have none of
his riding them. Then there was today's conversation.

It was my first day off in quite a while. Between classes, chores around the Carriage House, and working at the rec center, I just don't get much time off to enjoy myself. I woke up and the glorious weather called to me. I rushed through morning chores and slapped together a picnic lunch then went to tack up Aragorn for a day of riding on the Hawthorn Ringed Lands. It is days like this that I can almost see Fairies darting about in my peripheral vision. The peaceful atmosphere is better than a week of sleep for restoring my tired body and soul.

As we gallop, a power that is nearly euphoric surges through my body as Aragorn's movements and mine come into sync; the fresh winds rushing over us, awaking something deep in my soul. Drinking from any of the streams heightens all my senses and I can feel the life force of the forest tingling against my skin. The sighing of what remains of the leaves over us seem to hum a melodic underscore to the Aria of the birds. A day running wild and free on Hawthorn Ringed Lands is nothing short of bliss.

I was humming the tune with which a bird had been serenading me as I came into the Carriage House to find Rhys plopped at the kitchen table, eating from a plate of cookies I had baked the night before, surrounded by his usual stack of books. Upon seeing me, a broad smile flashed his perfect white teeth and glittered in his eyes. He immediately got up.

"There you are! Been riding have you? Well, come in and get warm. It turned colder than expected this afternoon. Have a seat by the fire and I'll get you some warm cider."

The good mood my ride had put me in could not be undone by the presence of Rhys Hawthorn and even made his fussing over me almost endearing. He had been right about the cold, I was shivering slightly and glad of the warmth of the fire as I settled into the velvet of one of the wing backed chairs. The after effects of being out on Hawthorn Ringed Land added to the aroma of the wassail Rhys had handed me that I greedily breathed in; letting it comfort my soul.

"Oh, so it's wassail? A bit weak for wassail isn't it?"

"It's not a traditional batch. I don't much fancy a fuzzy head."

"I suppose Constance Peters wouldn't. Did you enjoy your ride?"

"You know the answer to that."

"Yes, but I do love to converse with you aloud, you often manage to surprise me. And as much as I love nursery rhymes . . ."

I couldn't help but laugh. His attentiveness and earnest manner just made me happy. Reaching out to remove a rogue hair from my eyes, the lingering of his fingertips on the ridge of my cheekbone caused my breath to catch. Then he was up and running back to the kitchen with a sense of urgency.

"Oh, I almost forgot the cookies! I would call them gingerbread, but I know that isn't right. I do know that they are fabulous!"

"They are sorghum cookies. I got the recipe from Pippa."

"Dear cousin Pippa seems to have given you much."

I paused and stared at the dancing flames for a moment deep in thought. Pippa had saved my life in more than one way. I owed her and Barron more than I could ever repay. In the end all I could say was, "More than I deserve."

Rhys deposited the plate of cookies onto the marble topped table between the wing backed chairs and knelt on one knee; his left hand reaching out to turn my eyes to gaze into his.

"More than you deserve? Deserve, from the old French *deservir*, "to be worthy of, earn, merit". From Latin *deservire*, "to serve well". Coming to mean "be worthy of"circa 1300. I'd never say you are unworthy, and don't let me catch you saying or thinking such things either."

Unlike Pippa, Rhys tended to not voice his etymological musings. I couldn't help but blush at this one and I hoped that it read as the flush from riding against the wind that day. But I knew Rhys was paying particularly close attention to my thoughts which only made my blush deepen, causing him to laugh. I silently tossed about for a change of subject as I mentally recited Portia's speech on mercy from the Merchant of Venice.

"You are always surrounded by books when you come. What is this, the Hawthorn Family Library?"

A surprised look shook from where he knelt as he moved away to sit in the other wing backed chair.

"Surely you jest comparing this paltry collection of tomes to the Hawthorn Wordsmith Library."

"There really is a Hawthorn Wordsmith Library?"

My statement seemed to shock Rhys all the more.

"Don't tell me Pippa didn't show it to you? That surprises me. Surely she would have known how much you would have loved it. It is has grown exponentially since its heyday in Alexandria."

"The Hawthorn Wordsmith Library is the lost Library of Alexandria?"

"Not lost, just relocated. Several times throughout history. The City of Babel. The Hanging Gardens of Babylon. The City of Atlantis, Shangri La. Kunlun Mountain. Pompeii. Avalon. And now Hawthorn Heights. Bit anticlimactic that."

"I would indeed love to see it!"

"And I would show it to you, only cousin Pippa failed in her duties as the outgoing Hawthorn in Residence to meet with me and tell me her chosen location for its entrance. Nor did she entrust me with her key."

"What do you mean?"

"Whenever a Hawthorn Wordsmith takes residence at Hawthorn Heights, they move the entrance to the Hawthorn Wordsmith Library by making a new key. She didn't happen to leave you anything to pass on to me did she? I've been meaning to ask."

"No. Nothing. Why would she entrust me with such a thing?"

"Uh, uh, you are thinking of yourself as less than what you are again. I apologize for bringing it up and raising your hopes. But I shall keep looking to see where Pippa might have hidden it. She can't have taken it with her, and I am sure she had good reason to neglect her duties. Pippa never does anything without the most honorable of reasons."

The conversation turned to other delightful but inane topics. But now that Rhys has gone for the evening, I have this nagging feeling in the back of my mind. I know I was the one to bring up the Hawthorn Wordsmith Library, but I still couldn't shake the idea that somehow Rhys had come specifically to talk about it. Wordsmiths can lead the mind to an extent. And then there is the fact that Pippa hadn't entrusted Rhys with the Carriage House, essentially the care of the Hawthorn Ringed Lands, nor the location and key of the Hawthorn Wordsmith Library. I am starting to think that Pippa doesn't trust her cousin. If she doesn't trust Rhys then I don't really see how I can either.

October 31

Tonight was the Hawthorn University Halloween Bonfire. The bonfire is held in a field adjacent to the Hawthorn Estate, meaning the Estate is crawling with thrill seekers. There is no threat of them making their way to the Carriage House, but the animals are always a bit restless. Still, since I am a university student this year I decided to dress up and join the fun.

I admit, Vidette didn't really give me choice. It was all she could talk about for a month because Rhys' band, Elysian, was playing that night. She has a huge crush on the lead vocalist Takumi. Honestly, to look at her you'd take her for more of an acoustic guitar and tambourine kind of person, but I can always hear the strains of electric guitar solos coming from her ear buds. She has a particular love of J-rock bands of those odd costumed varieties. I also wouldn't take her for a screaming fangirl either, but when the band hit the stage in elaborate costumes I thought my ears were going to bleed from her screams alone.

I didn't really have a costume, so Vidette's roommate, Millicent, took me on as a challenge. Apparently she is something called a cosplayer. (I'd love to hear Pippa's take on that word.) She decided I should go as Joan of Arc, but her interpretation on it sort of reminded me of Don Quixote's hodge-podge of armor. It was a medieval dress and armor combination that I would have thought an impossible combination, but it worked.

Vidette and Millicent were dressed as characters from some anime they've been trying to get me to watch. To be honest, I just don't know if I can get into a kids cartoon that doesn't even speak English. Vidette swears I'll love it if I'll just give it a try. Still I have to admit they looked amazing. Millicent looked like a lavender haired female samurai of a similar ilk to my Joan of Arc, and Vidette looked like a turquoise haired gypsy warrior. (I secretly think if they'd gotten me to wear a wig, I'd have been another character from the anime, but I just couldn't do it.)   There were lots of costumes at the bonfire, but ours were some of the best in terms of design and quality. Millicent is studying costume design and I am sure I'll be seeing her work in all the movies someday.

Elysian is pretty amazing. The bassist Solomon and the lead vocalist Takumi write their songs which are full of musical variety, with clever and thought provoking lyrics. Turns out Millicent was the one to design the band's costumes as well. I'm really not sure what they were supposed to be, but they looked a bit like princes from another realm. All the swooning and sighing from the female attendants was more than enough clear indication that they were well received.

I had fun dancing and laughing with my friends for the first half of the night. About the time Elysian wrapped up their set my phone started ringing. It was a number I don't know. I am not the type to pick up a call if I don't know the number, but I can't shake the idea that it might be Barron or Pippa. I worked my way out of the crowd to quieter spot to try and hear, but when I answered, whoever it was had already hung up. I shook my head and made my way back toward the thick of the party when I was overwhelmed.

It was a scent that is burned into my soul. The scent of a certain cologne, booze, and a crowd. It reminded me of the night Conner tried to rape me and I felt panic creep into my heart. I knew it was irrational, but for some reason I started to run. Instinctively I was headed for the Carriage House. Tears burned in my eyes and the shadow and flame of the night blurred into a nightmarish Van Gogh around me.

When I heard footsteps quickly approaching I spun and threw my pursuer to the ground.

"Constance! Wait! It's me!"

Rhys' voice restored me to a bit of sanity, but I still blinked at him as if I couldn't recognize him.

"Constance, what happened? I sensed you were in distress. It felt like you ran into that guy that assaulted you. Are you okay?"

As Rhys spoke he stood and made his way to over to me. I just stood there trembling, so he tentatively put an arm around my shoulders. At his touch I melted into tears, wrapped my arms around him, and cried into his shoulder. Rhys patiently held me tight; stroking my hair to comfort me, whispering, 'It's okay. You're safe', until I managed to calm down.

"I'm sorry. I don't know what happened. I just had this sensation and I just panicked. I shouldn't be like this. I can beat that guy. I have beat that guy. Why am I even crying? This is so . . . so . . ."

"This is a panic attack. There is no reason to be ashamed Constance. Some scars to the soul are so

117

deep they haunt us no matter how strong we have become. Pippa once told me it is always better to run to people, not away from them, when the ghosts of our souls come to haunt us; that isolating ourselves is the worst thing we can do. Not that I am one to talk."

Rhys's words trailed off and he let go of me. I may not be a Wordsmith, but it was clear that he was failing to heed his own advice in the same moment he was giving it. As usual there was a war going on inside of Rhys; one being fought for the truth of his soul.

"Thank you Rhys. Thanks for coming to find me."

Rhys raised one eyebrow in a look of surprise. "You usually are annoyed when I show up uninvited. I debated about looking for you, but when I thought that man may have shown up again, I just couldn't . . ."

"Yeah, your showing up unannounced can be a bit annoying. But you came to fight off the ghost in my soul when no one else could have. That means a lot to me. The truth is since Pippa and Barron have left, that ghost has . . . well they were the light that helped to fight it off. So thanks, for saving me."

"I didn't really do anything."

"You did enough."

A huge smile spread across Rhys' face. Between the silver of the moonlight and his fantastical costume he really did look like a fairytale prince.

"Oh, don't go thinking I am a prince Miss Constance, for I assure you I am not. But there is none who would deny you bear all the marks of royalty. Indeed so fair a princess with skin of cream, hair of cinnamon, and eyes of emerald would have given Helen of Troy a fine rivalry. Now there is the smile I was missing."

My smile was at the absurdity of his statement of my rivalling Helen of Troy. Despite the fact I don't think a unanimous agreement of what the most beautiful woman in the world looks like could ever be reached, I am fairly average in most regards. Despite a Wordsmith's way with painting pictures with words, I am not exemplary nor deficient in any physical manner that would cause me to stand out in a crowd.

"Constance." Rhys drew out my name in the warning manner of a mother who's had enough and is about to start a countdown from three. "What have I told you about those kinds of thoughts?"

"Sorry mother," I quipped, imitating a testy preteen and rolling my eyes at him to make a point.

Rhys' laugh filled the forest around us. "Good, you are back to your normal self. Shall we return to the party? Your friends are looking for you. I would be most honored if you'd deign to let me escort you."

Rhys swept into a perfect bow as he spoke, then stood and offered me his elbow. I couldn't help but give a small laugh. He may well cause me any amount of confusion, but he can always make me smile. I accepted his elbow and we rejoined the party. Stepping into the firelight from the shadows of the forest I felt as if every eye in the field turned to look at us as we entered.

"What did you expect, I have the envy of Helen of Troy on my arm?" Rhys whispered into my ear.

I swear he loves to make me blush for his own amusement.

Vidette came running up looking a bit worried. "There you are! When I saw you run off, I . . . well I didn't know what to think. But I see I had no need to be worried."

"Lady Vidette as much as I am loath to part company with fair Constance, I have a duty to my band to which I must attend. Might I leave her in your care?"

"But of course! On one condition, you getting me a few minutes with Takumi at some point tonight."

Rhys laughed. "I shall see what I can do."

Kissing my hand he disappeared into the crowd.

Vidette gave me a suspecting look that gave way to a smirk. "Okay, so I knew you had some kind of relationship with our TA, but didn't have a clue it was that kind of relationship!"

"That kind of relationship? Oh, no. Trust me Vidette it isn't anything like that."

"Uh, huh. And just what kind of relationship do you think it is you have?"

"To be honest, I don't know. I sort of don't know if I can even trust him. That guy . . . he confuses me. I can't get a good read on him. He seems to be two things at once. It is like his soul is in confusion."

Vidette got a faraway gaze in her eye as if

120

she were seeing something beyond our immediate surroundings. "Someone once told me that at the heart of the human soul is a fire that can burn hot or cold, but it always has a distinct radiant light. Souls grow in the manner of trees, in that every experience is a ring around the fire of someone's heart. Some rings are transparent and others murky depending on the type of experience. What we see on the surface is the totality of their experiences illuminated by the fire of their heart. Sometimes the murky rings can make it difficult to see the truth about the fire of someone's heart, but those with great intuition can see the difference between those with cold fires in their hearts and the warm fires obscured by too many murky rings. Maybe you just have that kind of intuition Constance."

Given her dress, the firelight, and the manner of her speech Vidette could have passed for a gypsy fortune teller of old. I'd never noticed it before, but she too has a complex soul.

November 5th

Yesterday was chilled by the kind of cold my
grandmother would say settled in one's bones and
couldn't be easily shaken. Outside a grey rain had
made it impossible to distinguish the earth from
the sky; saturating anything that came in contact
with it. It was not the kind of day that invited one
to get out of bed, let alone venture outside. I'd
made myself get up and do my chores, but I decided not to trek to the university. It was just as well
I did as I got an emergency call from the rec center
about a burst pipe in the women's locker room
showers and was the only supervisor the on-duty
employees could get a hold of.

Cold and wet beyond the point of misery, I had
taken a long soak in the hot spring that serves as
the Carriage House's bath. (Seriously, what kind
of place has its own hot spring in this part of the
world? Not that I'm complaining, it is one of my
favorite things about living here.) A short while
later as I was making my way through my second bowl of French onion soup and third cup of
clove spice tea while skyping with Vidette about
the day's missed classes I heard the laundry room
door open. (Which reminds me, if I ever hear from
Pippa, I need to ask if it is okay to bring people to
the Carriage House. I'd love to show this place to
Vidette if no one else. And it would be nice to just
have a friend over to chat that isn't Rhys. Not that
I am certain Rhys is really a friend)

Rhys looked as soaked and miserable as I had

been. Actually, if possible he seemed more miserable and there was a jumpy quality to his movements despite the fact he just stood in the laundry room doorway dripping on the slate tile. I excused myself to Vidette and we hung up. I turned to look at the shivering Rhys, "There are some fresh dried towels in the dryer."

"Huh? Oh, thanks," Rhys mumbled, but remained where he was.

"Is everything ok?"

"Um, yeah. Well there are some sketchy looking blokes all around my loft and my security detail wanted me to get on Hawthorn Ringed Land as quickly as possible. I hate to do this to you, but I need to spend the night here."

For the first time I noticed the duffel bag slung over his shoulder. In all the time I've known Rhys I've never heard him mention, let alone seen, a security detail. It would make sense that he had one. I only knew Pippa's because I'd met Barron first. If a Wordsmith was seeking sanctuary on Hawthorn Ringed Land, something serious was going on.

"Oh, no. Don't worry. I am sure it is nothing. My security detail is just being cautious. I'm really sorry for barging in like this. I can sleep upstairs on the daybed in the loft."

"You are soaked through! And so is your bag. Come on, let's get your stuff in the dryer and you the hot spring. Then I've got some soup that will warm you up too!"

Rhys looked relieved almost to the point of tears. "Thank you Constance."

"Well, technically it is your house."

"But I've no right to your kindness. Yet you have never withheld it from me, even when I don't deserve it."

"I believe an edict was passed by the Hawthorn in Residence about saying such things. I wouldn't let him catch you either, he can be rather a stickler on that point"

Chuckling, a small smile appeared on Rhys' face and he relaxed and let me take his bag from him. I tossed him a towel from the dryer and urged him onto the hot spring. I set the secondary leather satchel that had been hiding under the duffle on the rough wood table by the outside door and dumped Rhys' damp things into the dryer to fluff. I rounded up some fresh sheets, pillows, and blankets and trundled them upstairs to the daybed in the loft.

The daybed freshly made up and Rhys' dried clothes delivered to the bath door, I found myself settled down with a book and Beatrix snuggled in my lap. The warmth of the fire with its gentle crackling coupled with the soft falling of rain nearly sent me off to sleep about the time Rhys made his reappearance. I was startled awake by the touch of a fleece blanket being tucked around me.

Rhys gave me a sad apologetic smile, "Sorry to wake you."

"I wasn't really asleep."

"You weren't awake either. And I was glad to see you getting rest. You've been looking a bit haggard lately. Don't misunderstand! Though there is something worn about your features and the way you carry yourself of late, you still wear it grace-

125

fully. Nothing could nullify your beauty. I just fear you are not getting enough rest."

I was still too drowsy to blush at his compliment. "I've been getting enough sleep. But I've had these odd dreams that seem to keep me from resting."

I knew my mind was moving unchecked among various thoughts; more thoughts than I would like to have shared, but I was too contented and close to the verge of sleep to care.

"I wish you had told me sooner. I have some tea that can help with that kind of sleep. But your dreams would account for the subject of your latest essay. We ask you to dig up your favorite mythology and you turn in a story very few know. The mythology of the Twin Worlds is common enough, but story of the Hawthorn is very archaic. Professor Julian was rather impressed you knew of it. I was relieved you managed to leave out the bit about Wordsmiths."

"I almost didn't. I just can't keep the story out of my head. It is like the story haunts my waking thoughts now."

"Do you mind sharing your dream with me?"

I went back and forth about it, but there was no reason not to tell him, he was already assessing and making sense of the words running through my mind. So I started from the beginning as I had earlier in this journal.

". . . and then two nights ago when I had the dream the speaker asked, "How many of the Hawthorn's five children were Hawthorn Wordsmiths?" I answered all Wordsmith's are Hawthorns. 'Foolish, shortsighted girl! Only one was a

126

Hawthorn Wordsmith!'"

Rhys had sat watching the flames as he soaked in my story. He turned and studied me for a bit as I fell silent.

"Judging by the snippets of appearance, plus the questions the storyteller was asking, it would seem you have dreamt of the Chief Elder Sage. It is an odd thing to be sure."

"Wait, the Chief Elder Sage? As in the Sages; the Faerie Kin that can read the soul and know the history of every inhabitant of the Twin Worlds? Why would I be dreaming of Sages?"

"Why indeed? You don't happen to be a Faerie Kin Sage do you? I thought not. It seems to me that the dream isn't really meant for you. So I think the better question is who is the dream meant for and why are you intercepting it? Then again those questions, and in particular the desired answers, are pretty specific for someone who wouldn't be close to a Hawthorn Wordsmith."

Nagging for my attention was a question that had unsettled me since I'd had that dream.

"What did the Chief Elder Sage mean about only one of the Hawthorn's children being a Hawthorn Wordsmith?"

"The Hawthorn had one son and four daughters. All of them inherited the Wordsmith ability. However, the title of Hawthorn Wordsmith and the chief responsibility for guiding the Faerie Kin in the World of Men was passed to the son; who in turn only had one son but two daughters. Every Hawthorn Wordsmith is the only son among the several daughters of the previous Hawthorn Wordsmith."

"Then what about Pippa? Does she have a brother I don't know about?"

"Pippa is an aberration. She is the only child of a Hawthorn Wordsmith, so she is the first daughter to hold the title. No one really knows why."

"Then if there is only one Hawthorn Wordsmith per generation, how are you a Hawthorn?"

"My mother is the sister of Pippa's father. She had two sons. Since some of the more traditional Faerie Kin are superstitious about a female Hawthorn Wordsmith, they voted that the closest male relative should be heir to the title. It's been a matter of dispute in the Faerie Kin Council since it was clear Pippa would be an only child."

"Are you saying that there are Faerie Kin, Wordsmiths, that don't want Pippa to be a Hawthorn Wordsmith?"

"Yes. And some very powerful ones at that. Though I think Pippa becoming the youngest Master Wordsmith in known history is proof she is powerful enough to hold the title. But when wolves think they've smelled blood. . ."

"Do you think that is why she and Barron disappeared?"

"I really couldn't say. I'm sorry I brought it up, this seems to have upset you. Would you allow me to make you some tea? I believe the correct blend is in Pippa's stores."

It was clear Rhys did not wish to discuss the matter further.

"Sure."

Rhys brewed me a pot of tea and it worked its magic quickly. In fact I don't remember how I got to bed. I do know that my dreams were wild for a time. I dreamt of Rhys tucking me into bed, kissing my forehead, and saying goodnight . . . or was it goodbye? Then there was a battle unlike any I have ever witnessed between Rhys and himself. I'd always known there was an almost duality about Rhys, but this dream left me on edge. The battle ended with one Rhys surrendering to the other. Then the dream went dark and I slept more soundly than I had for a very long time.

This morning when I awoke, Rhys was already sitting at the kitchen table drinking coffee, which was odd. The contents of his leather satchel were scattered across the table; an unending pile of essays, quizzes, and other assignments to be graded. As he greeted me something seemed different about him. But then he asked me to take some things in to Professor Julian because his security detail wanted him to stay on Hawthorn Ringed Land, so I suppose it was just stress. He sent me off with his usual warm smile and over pandering prose.

This whole latest encounter has me off kilter. I wish I could talk openly to someone about this. But, who would believe a story about Wordsmiths and Faerie Kin? And why haven't I heard from Pippa and Barron? It bothers me that I haven't. I miss them, yes, but I also have this feeling something is wrong. I know my concern is evident, as Vidette kept asking me at lunch if everything was okay. I nearly told her everything.

December 12

Rhys has been ever more different from the time he came to seek sanctuary at the Carriage House. His manner is more irritable. He barely has any interests outside of being at the Carriage House. I am surprised the band still lets him stay with them. (Well, he is unnaturally talented) He is almost constantly at the Carriage House now and he's been turning the place upside down.

He has his usual charm, but there is something off about it. He is looking for something, most likely the Hawthorn Wordsmith Library, and he thinks I am the one who knows where it is. My key to my journal even went missing for a while. It isn't that I didn't get that vibe off him before, but now there is a desperation about it. It's not like I was unaware that he wanted to charm information out of me, to make me blush for sheer amusement, or that he was frustrated at my ignorance, but before at least there was a warmth, a smile, a drop of sincerity to his flattery. Now he's cold. The words are the same, but the intent has changed. What truly happened that night? Does it have something to do with those men at Barron's flat?

The animals are acting even weirder toward him. In addition to being underfoot when Rhys is around, Chaucer and Beatrix are now sleeping in my room with me. Beatrix has even snuck into the Range Rover a couple of times.

No matter how many ways I come up with to lock the paddock, every morning there are four

chargers standing guard in the yard. They harass Rhys when he tries to enter the house when
I'm not there (and attempt to do so when I am).
As a result he waits till I'm home to visit. I know
it makes him uncomfortable that he can't move
freely about as he used to when I wasn't keeping a
close eye on him.

Still no word from Pippa or Barron. I really
wish I knew how to get a hold of them.

December 19

I really need to get ahold of Pippa or Barron. But, they didn't leave any numbers to call. My dad has some corporate numbers to call in case of a major emergency with any of the properties, but when I tried calling them no one seemed to know who I was talking about. I've been feeling isolated and my world is on its ear. I can't even believe the person I was almost grateful to this evening.

I had taken a nap this afternoon after classes. Rhys's band was playing a show at the Twisted Wick. (The owner, Jasper Reginald Basil, was a genius to turn that old gothic building just off the Hawthorn University campus into a quasi-free exchange library, art gallery, and coffee shop!) I was to meet Vidette and Millicent there, but I ended up oversleeping.

I had that dream again. But this time instead of the Chief Elder Sage asking me a question I was dismissed. It was the first time I've ever been able to explore any of our locations. This looked like the hall of mirrors in Versailles. Something familiar in the nearest mirror drew my attention. My heart nearly stopped. The face looking back at me from the mirror was Vidette.

I awoke with my heart racing. I grabbed my phone and tried to call Vidette but she didn't answer. That is when I noticed the time. She wasn't answering because the concert had already started. She probably couldn't hear me. I bolted out of the Carriage House like my tail was on fire, upsetting all of the animals in my charge in the process. I thought Raijin wasn't going to let me pass through the gateway out of Hawthorn Ringed Land.

Finding parking anywhere near the Twisted Wick was nearly impossible. I had to hike a good couple of blocks and by then I knew the concert had to be over. Still I couldn't get Vidette to answer her phone. I decided to take a shortcut through a couple of alleys. As I was trotting through the alley behind the Twisted Wick, I saw Rhys arguing with someone in the shadows. There were a couple of other people there as well. They looked like possible security, only they were acting as lookouts. One spotted me then the others, plus the one Rhys was arguing with, vanished.

I approached Rhys, but pulled up short when I could sense anger simmering in the air around him. He turned and gave me a hateful glare.

"Rhys? What's wrong?"

"Everything. Starting with Pippa and you!"

I was so shocked I started to back out of the alley into the crowded sidewalk by instinct. Rhys followed, grabbing my shoulders and shaking me violently.

"This is all your fault! I thought you and Pippa might be plotting, but it turns out you are just ignorant, dimwitted and useless. How can someone be so completely useless?"

I was too stunned to fight back. Someone knocked Rhys away from me and stood between us.

"Listen up. I don't know who you think you are but you are not to treat or speak to Constance that way. She is not ignorant, dimwitted, or useless.

You need to step off and cool off for a bit."

Rhys got this look in his eye that made me think he might unleash Babel on my defender. But he took a good look at the gathering crowd and disappeared into the shadows of the alley.

"Are you okay Constance?"

The man turned around and I nearly collapsed. It was Conner. I immediately took up a defensive position. Conner raised his hands and took two deliberate steps backward.

"I don't mean you any harm. I swear. I just want to know if you're okay?"

I managed to nod. A look of relief came over Conner's face and his stance relaxed.

"I'm glad. Look, Constance, I've been trying to find you. I've got something I really need to say to you, so if you have a minute?"

I again nodded, but my fighting stance only deepened.

"Okay, listen. I know that words are not going to undo what I did to you in the past. I know nothing can. But I've been going to narc anon for two years now and they encourage us to make amends as best as possible. I've managed to talk to almost everyone, but I just couldn't bring myself to talk to you."

I simply kept staring at Conner. I knew what he was trying to do, but the truth is in that moment I didn't want him to apologize. I didn't want him to be the one who had chased off Rhys. I know Rhys told me not to mistake him for a prince and he may have been a different person of late, but when my worst enemy just chased off my supposed prince, well the world was spinning around

135

in a free fall.

"Look nothing can excuse my actions. I am not expecting forgiveness. In fact I wouldn't even ask for it, but I want you to hear my story. When I met you I was an angry person. So unbelievably angry. Not that it matters, but I was angry at my parents for separating and being more worried over who got custody of the Rembrandt and Degas than me. I'd tried numbing the anger with drugs, and when that didn't work I took it out on you. The truth is, I was attracted to you. You were smart and nice and pretty. But I was so messed up inside, it all just came out wrong. And when you rejected me, I snapped."

Conner was trembling and his eyes pleaded with me for something I don't think I can ever give.

"I am so sorry I hurt you Constance. I am sorry for trying to rape you. I am sorry for instigating the bullying. If I could go back and change it, I would. If I could stop myself before. . . that's the only way I could make up for what I did. But I can't. And what haunts me is that you bear the weight of my sins. I know you are suffering be-cause of my actions and that . . . I just want you to know that . . . Oh, God, there just aren't words for this . . . I knew there wouldn't be. . . but I just . . . You saved my life, Constance. If you hadn't had the strength to confront me, no one would have stopped me. I wouldn't have come face to face with the consequences of my actions. I wouldn't have found narc anon and my counselors. The truth is, I owe you my life and I ruined yours. I can't expect forgiveness, but I do want you know my gratitude. Thank you Constance. "

The wet and warmth of tears was on my face; but their source was uncertain. They could easily have been tears of rage, pain, sorrow, or countless other emotions that had no other way of expressing themselves in that moment. Conner was sincere. Of that I was certain. But I had no voice. My only response was to finally relent my fighting stance.

"I doubt you ever want to see me again, but here."

Conner was holding out a business card, but he was conscious of his distance from me. He was making an effort and my body reacted by taking his card. He worked for a high end car repair shop.

"This is going to sound lame, but if you ever need anything, call. I'll do anything to help you."

Shoving his hands into his jacket pockets and ducking his head, Conner disappeared into the crowd outside the Twisted Wick.

I never did find Vidette. Millicent said she'd suddenly had to go home, but she never would answer her phone. This day has been . . .

I don't know. My ally is my enemy. My foe is my friend. My eyes have been opened to the idea that Vidette may well be Faerie Kin; she was the confidant I needed but couldn't even see.

When I met Pippa, I found out that the world wasn't at all the boring straight forward place I had thought it was. But before even meeting Pippa, I had learned the hard way that it certainly wasn't the safe place everyone mistakes it to be. I remember something Pippa once told me.

"I think all of us know that true reality is not what we think we see around us. Just because one or two masks come off on occasion, the entirely of the masquerade still remains. Masks can only be removed one or a few at a time and most of us don't want to see what exists below. Much of the time we want to see the safe and secure false reality portrayed by the mask, so sometimes even when the masks are off, we refuse to look at the true unsecure reality. And other times we look at the true reality and it is so far from what we could ever imagine that we don't even know at what we are looking. You should always remember that not seeing what lies beneath the mask does not make the true reality any less real and there is always the hope that what lies beneath the mask is a better reality than the one you can see."

I am not sure what to think at this point. All I know is that as much as removing masks would give some clarity, I am growing more terrified of what I will find beneath; the promise of hope seems hollow.

December 23

Writing this down is going to tempt writer's cramp, but if I don't give some order to the maelstrom of my thoughts I don't think I'll even really understand what has happened.

It started the morning after writing my last entry. I'd been sitting in my favorite wing backed chair writing and eating my sorrows. Finishing putting my thoughts on paper, I snuggled under a blanket and fell asleep staring into the fire.

The sound of my journal hitting the slate floor jolted me awake. There was a pale grey early morning light coming in through the windows. My heart was racing and I almost missed the gentle pressure on my knee that alerted me to the presence of Beatrix. I looked at the giant French Lop who blinked back at me for a few seconds then nudged the fallen journal. As I stooped to pick up the journal, something along the fore edge of the pages caught my eye in the dim light.

Pippa had a huge collection of books with elaborate fore edge paintings, holding any manner of hidden messages. It had never occurred to me that there could be one on my journal. But now that I can see it, I don't know how I ever missed it. It has two large doors that looked vaguely familiar bookending an ornate key that was identical to the one for my journal. Along the blade of the key was beautiful script lettering: Sophia Elaine Phillipa Hawthorn.

I pulled the key out from under my shirt and

inspected it in the cool morning light. There was elaborate scroll work along the blade, but no letters. I wracked my brain to think of where I had seen those doors before. As I stared off into the distance I became aware of Chaucer staring at me. He cocked his head to one side and then looked from me to something behind me. Turning around the truth hit me like a ton of bricks. Of course, it was the main entrance to the Carriage House. In all the time I've been coming here I've never seen it opened!

Only stopping in the laundry room to don a hoody and socks of questionable cleanliness, shove my feet in some work boots, and grab my coat, I ran outside. I've never really looked at the main entrance doors before. I knew that they were a masterpiece of wrought iron and wood, but I'd missed the story that they told.

Everything about the Carriage House told a story if you took the time to see it. The main entrance door told the story of the Hawthorn. A Hawthorn tree dominated the scene were any number of creatures from the World of Men and the World of Faerie; all watching a young boy nestled in the branches of the Hawthorn. The expression of the boy's face clearly relayed his being in the middle of an exuberant telling of some tale. Flopped open across the branch next to the boy was a book. The book had a clasp lock that looked like the one on my journal, complete with a functional keyhole.

Trembling I pulled the chain over my head and placed the key into the keyhole. However, my excitement was short lived as the key refused to

140

turn. I tried until my bare hands were numb with the cold. My cheeks and nose were burning with the cold of the December day, but I wouldn't give up. I was too close. I pulled my journal I'd stashed in my hoody front pocket and looked at the fore edge painting again. Why would Pippa write her name on the key? She'd always told me that names were powerful and that Faerie Kin don't easily entrust them to others. So why? Of Course!

Taking hold of the key I softly spoke aloud, "Sophia Elaine Philippa Hawthorn."

The key turned without any further opposition. Of their own accord the massive doors swung inward, creaking their complaints of having to open after being so long out of use.   I had to shield my eyes; the giant gold and precious stone encrusted seal of the Hawthorn Wordsmith adorning the wall beyond the doors was brightly reflecting the weak morning light.

Rustling at my feet drew my attention to Chaucer and Beatrix who had followed me outside. It wasn't an unusual occurrence for Beatrix who spends hours outside exploring, but Chaucer only ventured outside on exceptionally nice days. I guess he sensed an adventure, for he and Beatrix wasted no time rushing down the stone stairway beyond the carved porphyry archway beneath the Seal of the Hawthorn Wordsmith.

Pausing, I removed the key from the door and slid the chain back over my head, securing the key beneath my hoody. I tried to close the doors, but they stood resolute. I whispered Pippa's true name again, but the doors would not be moved. Shrugging, I gave up and followed after the rabbits. Be-

141

hind me I could hear the doors closing themselves. I guess enchanted doorways and portals are persnickety.

I truly wish I had the ability to describe the Hawthorn Wordsmith Library, but I doubt Shakespeare could do it justice. Well, maybe he could, he was the most famous Master Wordsmith to ever live. The sheer size of the Library is unbelievable. I think it is spread out for the majority of the Hawthorn Ringed Land. Or perhaps the Hawthorn Ringed Land is the size of the Library. For someplace that is supposedly underground, there is an abundance of natural light allowing for the growth of plants and flowers of colors I've never seen before; all fed by the natural springs flowing from exquisitely carved or naturally formed fountains. These garden spaces meandered throughout the Library which was almost as much of a museum as it was a library. Artworks of unimaginable beauty were everywhere. Books and manuscripts in every tongue in the Word of Men and the World of Faerie lined shelves or stood in stacks on large tables.

Laughing I realized that Pippa's organized chaos in the Carriage House was genetic. It would seem generations of Hawthorn Wordsmiths have utilized the pile method of organization. I spent the entire day exploring the library. When I got hungry I simply picked fruit from the trees growing there. In retrospect, I probably should have been more cautious of what I put in my mouth. It is just that the peace down there was so complete.

The only sounds were that of running water and otherworldly birdsong. I heard rustling just out of sight from time to time, but the only time

I ever saw anything it was Chaucer and Beatrix. They lazily explored in my vicinity wherever I roamed.

To say the entirety of the Library was peaceful would be a lie. There were some places that made my skin crawl. They were darker places with little natural light and their contents were contorted with leering gargoyles standing guard. Paranoia always filled me when I was in those places and I started at every little sound; imagining the shadows moving to conceal things in the dark. I had no desire to know what kind of things were kept in those places.

But in the light places I found myself picking up any number of books and manuscripts. I'd sprawl out on the thick grass or perch on an obliging bench, chair, or ledge to read whatever my hand had found to pick up. At some point late in the day I curled up on an piece of furniture that could have been an enormous overstuffed fainting couch covered in the most sumptuous fabric. It kind of reminded me of the wing backed chairs in the Carriage House. It was there I fell asleep.

My dreams ran the breadth and width of the world; in fact I think I may have leapfrogged from place to place across the whole of the Twin Worlds. They were at once glorious and terrifying. It was unlike anything I'd ever experienced. I was fully aware of myself as an outsider to the dreams. The longer I hopped from dream to dream the more I found myself dreaming of those I knew. My family seemed to be having some interesting dreams that I'll have to analyze later, but the dreams of my friends were upsetting. Pippa and Barron were in a frantic state to get somewhere. They kept saying how they should have figured it out sooner. Vidette was on the run. It was like watching a horror movie with my best friend as the one being pursued by the beast. Then there was Rhys. He was hunting himself. And he was hunting me.

I was awoken by the sound of my phone ringing. I'd quite forgotten it was in my pocket. Groggily I clumsily fished it out and dropped it onto the floor. My eyes barely able to focus, I scrambled to get a hold of it. Getting a good look at the callers ID I was fully awake. It was Pippa.

"Constance, where are you?"

It was in that moment that it occurred to me that I had no idea where I was. I hadn't taken any manner of precaution to mark my path. I could be lost in the Library for days, not that I'd mind too terribly. But there was something urgent in Pippa's voice.

"I'm in the Hawthorn Wordsmith Library, only I don't know exactly where."

Pippa laughed. "It doesn't surprise me. And it's just as well. Put me on speaker."

I did as she asked and she spoke some words I didn't recognize and a map materialized on the couch next to me.

"You can't go back through the main entrance. It isn't safe. You need to go out the back door. Tell the map, 'Ducere ad portam quod non permittit intrare'. Be careful, Constance."

"Pippa! What's going on?"

The phone beeped and Pippa was gone. Chaucer and Beatrix sat looking at me as I just stared at the phone as if it would magically reconnect me to Pippa by my willing it to do so. I heaved a sigh and grabbed the map.

"Ducere ad portam quod non permittit intrare."

I felt a thrill as I spoke the words. Pippa had always told me that Words of Power were merely the right words for a given situation. She'd always known I'd secretly wished for a spell. She didn't exactly give me a spell, just the Latin asking to be lead to the gate that allows no one to enter. It was still exhilarating to watch a navy and bronze line thread its way across the map from where I sat to the back door of the Library.

Picking up my phone I checked the time out of curiosity. The time was of little importance, but the date was December 21st. I'd been in the Library more than 24 hours! I sprang off the couch upsetting the stack of illuminated manuscripts I'd been reading. I paused to quickly stack them back up before following the map. I was grateful our way took us past some fruit trees and I hungrily ate as my long eared companions and I made our way out of the library.

We emerged out the front door of the Hawthorn Estate ruins. I dithered on the charred front steps. Pippa had discouraged me from going out the main entrance which lead to the Carriage House. My intuition told me not to go back there. But I didn't know where to go. I couldn't go home. I didn't want my family to be in danger. As I stood vacillating, I heard someone call out my name. Looking up I saw Rhys trotting toward me.

I ran.

I didn't have a destination I just ran.

I remember ducking through a pair of Hawthorn sentinels onto Hawthorn Ringed Land, it
is only natural to seek sanctuary in a sanctuary I
suppose. I also recall making every effort not to
run back to the Carriage House. Rhys pursued me
at a preternatural pace, getting ahead of me to cut
me off. I went to dodge him but he grabbed my
arm. I reacted but he was ready for it; he bounded
away but still so as to block me. There was a look
of concern in his eyes.

"Constance! What on earth is going on? You
disappeared, no one could find you! Are you
okay?"

"What do you care? I'm nothing but useless,
ignorant, and dimwitted," I spat.

A look of contrition bowed Rhys' head. "I am
so sorry about the other night. I was frustrated,
but I never should have said those things to you.
I came to apologize but you were gone. I've been
out of my mind looking for you."

"I didn't mean to disappear, but I didn't really want to see you anyway. I'm sorry. No I am
not sorry. You know who stepped in to save me
from you? Conner! Conner! Of all the people in
this world it was Conner! And what he told me
afterwards . . . what I had to go through . . . alone
thanks to your selfishness. . . I don't ever want to
see you again."

"Constance, please don't say that. I'm sorry. I
am so very sorry. If I'd had any idea who that was.
. ."

"Save it. I really don't want to hear another
word out of you."

"Where have you been Constance?" A greedy

gleam came into his eye. "You found it. You found the entrance to the Library. You figured out the key. Show me. Please. I will make everything up to you if you will just show me."

I stood just staring at him when a voice called out to me.

"Don't Constance. Get away from him. That is not Rhys Hawthorn."

Without even verifying the owner of the voice I ran as fast as I could in its direction as I shouted. "I know."

I wasn't fast enough and the false Rhys caught me around the waist and put a gun to my head.

"A gun? Bit of a weak tactic for a Wordsmith," I growled.

"Well, I am dealing with the weak minded. Put down your weapon and come out where I can see you."

Barron dropped out of a tree and leaned against its trunk rather nonchalantly. "And why would you be afraid of little old me when I am with a Master Wordsmith and a true Hawthorn Wordsmith at that."

Pippa materialized on a lower hanging branch of a nearby tree. "Hello Eagan. Seems my little protégé figured you out."

"You may look alike, but Rhys wouldn't drink coffee if he was on the verge of dehydration and he does have a conscience," I snapped. "As for you, I just didn't have a name for you. Plus I knew you would read my journal. Thanks for returning the key by the way. And Barron, thanks for the books of poetry and nursery rhymes, I got plenty of use out of them."

"Now Eagan," Pippa cooed like a kindergarten teacher trying to settle a spat between five year olds, "why don't you let Constance go and you and I can have a little discussion about your father's plans now that these have been foiled. Discussion. Middle English, from the Latin root discutere, meaning 'investigate'. Right Constance? "

"Who says they've been foiled?"

Eagan's hand plunged into my hoody and yanked the chain with my key. After several seconds of choking I felt the chain give. A thunderous bang deafened me as the world became nothing but pain. Eagan had shot me.

Everything was distant. There were voices calling my name and begging me to open my eyes. I wanted to, but I couldn't. Nothing was responding to me. I felt as if my soul were slipping away from my consciousness. And that's when I heard it. I heard Bethesda- the Heavenly Word of Healing. The second most common Heavenly Word of Power next to Babel.

Peace ushered my soul back to its proper place and a light filled my body with more sensations than I shall ever be able to feel again. I felt someone's forehead pressed against mine and could hear the barely audible final syllables of Bethesda.

My eyes opened and fought to focus on the face before them. It was Rhys. The true Rhys. I reached up to touch his face and he instantly pulled me up into a crushing embrace.

"Thank the Father of the Twin Worlds, I didn't know if Bethesda would work for me. Oh, Constance, I felt your mind go quiet . . . Vidette said your soul was slipping from this realm . . . I couldn't . . ."

Rocking back and forth Rhys didn't release me from his hold until it was apparent I couldn't breath. Even then he continued to support me as I was yet to be able to support myself.

"Rhys where have you been these past months?"

"In prison. But that is a long story and there is something I must do. But I can't go without telling you something more important Constance. Thank you for knowing Eagen wasn't me. You and Pippa are the only ones who ever saw us as individuals. Even my parents just regarded us as interchangeable pawns in their schemes for power. But Pippa always knew who I was, and she always encouraged me to be true to my soul. But I didn't know how. Not till I met you Constance. It was you who fanned the flames in my soul to outshine its murky rings. Constance, I love you."

Rhys pulled me in close and kissed me softly. For an instant I recoiled. I hadn't let anyone kiss me since Conner. But in reality I had barely let anyone touch me since Conner either. No one, except Rhys. I had never recoiled from his touch. And so I let myself melt into the warmth of his kiss to sincerely return with my own.

Tasting the salt of tears mixed in with our kiss, when my lips parted from Rhys' I could see tears coursing down his face. To my bewilderment he handed me over to Vidette, whom I hadn't even realized was there. Kneeling, Rhys caressed my face, placing a lingering kiss on my forehead then left without a word.

Vidette sat biting her lower lip as she inspected me with worry filled eyes. "Are you really going to be okay?"

"I don't know."

"Do we need to get you to a doctor?"

"What? No. Physically, I'll be fine. But . . . Vidette help me follow him."

"Can you even stand?"

"Won't know till I try."

"I don't think you should be moving."

"Vidette something is wrong. Please help me!"

Vidette finally nodded her consent and we began the awkward dance of getting me to my feet. I could still feel the power of Bethesda working. I knew it wouldn't be long before I was better than new. But at the time I could barely put one foot in front of the other.

The thick underbrush made our way difficult, but slowly we pressed on toward the sounds of fighting. Pausing on the edge of a clearing it was difficult to process what we were seeing. Rhys had thrown himself between Pippa and Eagan, shoving Pippa backward. The sound of the winds of the earth swirling above knocked Vidette and me off our feet. Barron appeared out of nowhere and shoved something onto Pippa's head before shielding her as if from an atomic blast.

The only thing that I could tell for sure was that Rhys was using Heavenly Words of Power and Eagan was terrified. Eagan tried to run, but his feet became rooted in the earth- literally. His entire body contorted, twisting outward into the form of a Hawthorn tree. To my horror Rhys arms and legs were elongating and transforming into a

Hawthorn as well.

"Rhys!"

There was no way Rhys could have heard my call over the windstorm, but he turned to look at me. There were tears still in his eyes as he called out something to me. I couldn't hear him, but I know he was telling me he loved me one last time. A clap of thunder shook the clearing and twin Hawthorns stood at its center.

What just happened?

The question repeated itself over and over in my mind.

I was vaguely aware of Barron checking Pippa up one side and down the other as she removed what looked like headphones.

"Barron I'm fine. I'm a Hawthorn Wordsmith not a tree. Calm down!"

"Are you sure, are you absolutely sure that Word of Power had no effect on you? Your skin is looking a little too dry and barkish."

Pippa took Barron's face in her hands. "Barron I promise I am fine. That Word of Power is bound to an individual by that person's true name and Rhys doesn't know mine."

"But he's not a Master. . . Pippa did it even cross your mind that he might. . .'

"You're right, Rhys wasn't strong enough to properly use the Heavenly Word of Power. Thank you for your quick thinking, it may very well have saved me."

Barron kissed Pippa fiercely. I'd never seen them kiss and some part of me melted, some part of me squealed in delight, and some part of me was sad beyond words. I felt tears sliding down

151

my cheeks.

Barron wrapped Pippa in his arms and kissed the top of her head. "There is no hole Ankou can hide in that I won't find him as it is, but if he . . . if you . . . " Pippa embraced the unnerved Barron. Laying her head on his chest, the tension relaxed out of his body. "I can't go through that nightmare again. I only survived the last time because of you. When I lost everything, I found you. If I lose you, then I am truly lost."

When they finally separated they turned to look at the aftermath of Rhys' Heavenly Words of Power.

"No Barron, you can't turn them into firewood. They are Hawthorns after all."

Barron grimaced and turned away from the Twin Hawthorns. Seeing me, he shook his head and gave a sigh. "I'm starting to see the family resemblance between you two."

Pippa gave him a quizzical look then followed his gaze over to me. "I guess we have some ex-plaining to do. Explain. Early 15th Century from Latin explanare, to make plain or clear. But don't think you are off the hook for that skin crack mis-ter."

Pippa knelt next to me and gave me a hug. "I am so proud of you Constance. Proud, from Old French prud 'valiant,' based on Latin prodesse 'be of value.' You are indeed valiant and possessing great worth. I am so sorry for what you had to go through though. If I could, I would have shielded you from all this, but I'm afraid you were always going to be drawn into this conflict. And I hate to tell you, but it isn't over yet."

I had nothing else to voice but the relentless question in my mind. "What just happened?"

Barron answered.

"Rhys used the Heavenly Word of Power that originally turned the Hawthorn human. It is also used to turn Wordsmiths that have gone rogue and wreaked irreparable damage on the world by the misuse of their power, like Adolf Hitler, back into Hawthorn trees."

Barron paused in his explanation. Standing behind Pippa, Barron's eyes shot daggers at the Twin Hawthorns, revealing his barely kept anger. I've rarely seen him like that. Normally when he gets frustrated or irritated, it merely ruffles him on the surface and he quickly calms after only a moment. But his fury in that moment came from deep in his soul. The first time I'd seen that icy fire in his eyes, so full of rage and cold determination, was after he found out about what Connor had done to me. I was acutely aware of the smoldering incensed fervor in his voice as he continued his explanation.

"But Rhys isn't nearly powerful enough to wield Heavenly Words of Power. However, he's clever. Today is the Winter Solstice and this is Hawthorn Ringed Land that hosts the most powerful portal magic in the World of Men, the Hawthorn Wordsmith Library. He used those to his advantage. Still, I'm certain he knew he would never escape his own spell. He didn't have the skill to separate himself from it."

"But why?"

"My uncle, Ankou Eris, wanted them to succeed me as the Hawthorn Wordsmith. The plan was to locate the Library and steal the Heavenly Word of Power to use on me," Pippa whispered.

Visibly bristling, every muscle in Barron's body looked tensed and ready to unleash violence on the world with the slightest provocation; it was a jarring reminder that he was an Argonaut Faerie Kin.

"Ankou has tried before to kill Pippa, back in the Hindu Kush, comes to mind. You'd be amazed how many Faerie Kin terrorist groups that man has control of by now. He's been trying to leverage support for his sons to be named the Hawthorn Wordsmith; arguing that the Hawthorn Wordsmith must be male; that as long as it was a grandson of a Hawthorn Wordsmith, they'd have a right to claim the title. They've managed to back the other two living Hawthorn Wordsmiths, Pippa's father and grandfather, into a corner over the matter of naming her a Hawthorn Wordsmith."

Replacing the flames of ice, a proud gleam glittered in his eye and a smirk appeared on his countenance as Barron tousled Pippa's hair, causing her to frown up at him. Barron teasing Pippa was a familiar scene; one that told me the threat of him releasing his inherited legendary ability to accomplish impossible feats had passed.

"But Pippa keeps managing to overpower and outwit Ankou and his supporters on the Faerie Kin Council. She is the Hawthorn Wordsmith and the youngest known Master Wordsmith. Her power is rather incredible, even by Wordsmith and Faerie Kin standards. Ankou got it in his head that the only way to defeat Pippa was by turning her back into a tree. Rhys agreed to find the Word of Power, but apparently he always intended to use it on Eagan. He knew that with him and his brother gone, there would be no one left to fight Pippa for the title of Hawthorn Wordsmith."

Pippa's hand moved atop Barron's hand that had returned to rest on her shoulders. It is still odd to me that they are so comfortably affectionate. I'd watched them imitate magnets, both attracting and repelling each other, for almost two years. After they were official, it seemed every touch, while charged with passion, was tinged with caution. But Barron and Pippa's mannerisms as Pippa took up the explanation made me wonder what all had happened while they were away.

"But turning me into a tree wasn't Uncle Ankou's only scheme in play. So I arranged it that Rhys could come and be the Hawthorn in Residence while we did some investigating. Ankou was thrilled, thinking I'd played into his plans. He was certain that I had a blind spot for Rhys. He never dreamed that it was he who had the blind spot. As I couldn't just disappear with the key, I consulted with an old friend from the World of Faerie and he bespelled a journal and key to give to you Constance. I knew you'd figure it out when the time was right. I also knew you would be good for Rhys. I just didn't think you'd have that strong an influence so quickly. I was certain I could trust you both."

"I never trusted that two faced kid, and I was right. How on earth did he get that Heavenly Word of Power?"

Given Barron's volatile state, I had to applaud

Vidette for her courage.

"I got it for him."

Barron and Pippa seemed to notice Vidette for the first time. Dropping to his knee next to Pippa so as to be eye to eye with Vidette, Barron demanded, "What do you mean?"

"A couple of nights ago I saw who I thought was Rhys lighting into Constance out behind the Twisted Wick. It was the first time I could clearly see his soul and I knew that he wasn't Rhys. I decided to follow him. "

"You saw his soul?" Barron asked.

"She's a Sage, Barron. If I'm not mistaken the heir to the Chief Elder Sage. Impressive. Go on, dear. Don't mind him. He's had a terrible fright and its left him vexed. Vexed. Late Middle English. Having a Latin root, vexare 'shaken, disturbed'."

Barron shot Pippa a disapproving look, then reached out to touch her as if still needing proof she was okay; however he remained quiet as Vidette continued.

"I followed Eagan and he led me to where Rhys was being held prisoner. I tried to free Rhys but he said it was too dangerous. If he was found having escaped, his twin brother would go straight after Constance. Rhys couldn't overpower Eagan, so he agreed to let his brother take his place to get the location of the Library only after Eagan swore a Wordsmith Oath not to hurt Constance in return. But he also told me he had a way to beat his brother, but he needed my help. He needed me to follow Constance. He told me a bit about the Hawthorn Wordsmith Library, what he needed from there, and how to find it. To be honest I didn't know what I was doing, but the state of his soul was Sincerus, Latin for 'clean and pure'. A truly Sincerus Soul is rare, so I chose to trust him."

Pippa nodded her approval and Barron rolled his eyes. Pippa prompted Vidette to continue with a question. "How did you get in the Library?"

"I didn't think I'd have the chance, but then Constance couldn't get the doors to close. I snuck in after her and they closed behind me."

"So the doors remained open for you and the Library let you leave with the Heavenly Word of Power. Shall I never be free from the machinations of minds who regard themselves as superior? I am going to have to have a long talk with that scaffy old wizard. Scaffy. Scots meaning, 'good for nothing'. Oh, how I do love Scots. Anyway, you took it back to Rhys?"

"Yes. While I was on my way Eagan posing as Rhys called concerned about the disappearance of Constance. I went to help him search. When I met him I got a good look at his soul and saw it was Malevolentia- full of ill intent. I ditched him when I could and ran to free Rhys who'd been studying the spell I stole for him. I knew we were running out of time. But it took too long and we arrived in time to see Eagan shoot Constance. But if I had known Rhys meant to sacrifi. . ."

"You can't blame yourself for the self-ordained fates of others. Ordain. From the Latin ordinare, 'put in order, arrange, dispose, appoint'. As a Sage you should know well that in the end, you can save someone from everything but themselves."

Vidette solemnly nodded then gave a shiver.

"Come on Pippa let's get out of this cold."

"Great idea Barron," Pippa replied, helping Vidette up off the ground, "I think a roaring fire, some sorghum cookies, and a bit of wassail are in order."

Barron gently lifted me from the ground and carried me. As we walked in the direction of the Carriage House I looked back at the Hawthorn that had once been Rhys until it was out of view.

"I am truly sorry Constance."

Barron spoke quietly as we followed behind a chattering Pippa and Vidette.

"I sent you to Pippa in hopes of helping you, but in the end you've . . . well gotten more than you or I bargained for. Not the least of which is having been shot and had your heart broken all in one day."

"I won't say I'm not upset or that my heart isn't aching. But I never knew if I could even trust Rhys till he saved my life. I care about him deeply. But, I can't say that I loved him- at least not in the way Pippa defines love. And as for being shot, well, I wasn't without fault either. But Barron, I wouldn't say sending me to Pippa has done me anything but good."

I wrapped my arms around Barron's neck. Despite my brave words, everything that had happened caught up to me and I started to weep. Barron just let me cry all the way back to the Carriage House.

June 21

Today Pippa and Baron were married! I was the maid of honor and I finally got to meet Dane Ford who was the best man. It turns out Dane Ford had figured out Ankou's plans and wanted the Faerie Kin world to think him dead so he could go after Ankou. He finally revealed himself to Barron. The two of them had been working together to figure out what Ankou was up to but got caught by Pippa. (Which explains that one fight I thought was going to be the end of Pippa and Barron.)

It also turns out that Dane Ford was Pippa's biological grandfather on her mother's side! Pippa never even knew her mother was adopted. And Pippa's mother had a twin who was my maternal grandmother. That makes me and Pippa first cousins once removed and Dane Ford my great grandfather. Apparently, Dane never knew about his daughters until long after he became Pippa's primary head of security and Pippa's parents told him the truth. Yeah, it all has my head spinning.

As for the wedding, it was a small ceremony in the Hawthorn Wordsmith Library. It was absolutely beautiful; you couldn't ask for a more perfectly romantic place to get married! Pippa was a stunning bride and Barron couldn't stop smiling.

But I've been a bit melancholy. Rhys has been on my mind a lot lately. I barely knew him, but he sacrificed himself for Pippa and put himself at his brother's mercy for me. I have so many things I wish I could ask him to help me reconcile the events of last fall in my mind.

I found myself wandering out to the paddock to pet Aragorn. He always seems to understand my moods and makes me feel better. As I was petting his nose explaining my feelings, Aragorn knelt on one knee as if he wanted me to climb on. I did, without a second thought to my expensive and gorgeous dress Pippa had hand made for me. I heard a yell and turned to see Vidette running toward us. I confided that I wished she could come, but . . .

Aragorn gave a whinny and Nerida trotted over to Vidette. She wasn't really comfortable around horses, so Vidette simply reached out to pet the soft velvet of the mare's nose. The beautiful blue roan knelt down for Vidette and my friend finally gave into the adventure of the moment and climbed up onto Nerida. Aragorn set off across the Hawthorn Ringed Land in a smooth canter that in no way threatened to unseat me. I could hear the hoof falls of Nerida, Raijin, and Matilda behind me.

I really didn't care where we went it just felt good to be riding. As we rode I listened to the birdsong and bubbling brooks. Entering a rather large open pasture, Matilda challenged Aragorn to a race. I gave my blood bay stallion his head and we chased after the black buckskin mare. We pulled up at the tree line and waited for Nerida and patient Raijin to catch up. Holding on for dear life should Nerida decide to join in our fun, Vidette's expression and gestures made me laugh.

Finally, Aragorn delivered me to the clearing

where Rhys and Eagan stood as twin Hawthorn trees. I hadn't been back since that day, and the memory squeezed my heart. I guessed I'd subconsciously made my way there. I slipped off Aragorn, but could only stand next to him in the safety of the curve between his shoulder and his neck. Aragorn stood still and let me borrow his strength. Slowly I summoned my courage. One slow and deliberate step at a time, I crossed over to the tree that had once been Rhys Eris. No, he was Rhys Hawthorn. Even Pippa said he'd earned the name.

Trembling, I touched my fingers to the bark of the tree and breathed, "Rhys."

I could almost imagine his arms wrapping around me from behind and placing a kiss on the top of my head. Only I wasn't imagining. I knew I wasn't.

"Get your hands off Constance you rogue!"

Someone snatched me from Rhys's arms and stood between us. It was Aragorn. Well sort of. It was a tall breathtakingly handsome man who had to be from the World of Faerie. But I somehow knew it was my horse Aragorn. For one thing his hair was the same blood bay color and he had the same fiery energy about him.

I stared uncomprehending, blinking at the sight of Rhys who wasn't Rhys and Aragorn who wasn't Aragorn. How was this even possible? How was it that my horse was a man and my friend a ghost? (Or spirit I suppose.) The world no longer made any sense and has yet to recover any.

As my mind was reeling from impossible that stared me in the face, a strong presence took up a position beside me. I looked over so see a man

163

who would have towered over Barron and made him look like a pushover. He had a familiar kind of gentle strength that made you feel secure.

"Raijin!?! Aragorn!?! What is going on here?"

'Aragorn' shot Rhys a look of emnity that might as well have been poison. He then looked at me with a gentle countenance of contrition.

"I am sorry Constance, I brought you here because you were sad. I knew you were needing closure. I did not think this man would have a presence on this side."

I stepped toward the ephemeral Rhys. To be honest I am not sure how I knew it was Rhys; his whispy form came in and out of focus. When in focus his features looked nothing like Rhys as I remembered him. I've decided that what I recognized was Rhys' soul.

"Is that really you Rhys?"

"Yes. This is my tree spirit form on the World of Faerie."

I reached out and touched Rhys' face. I wouldn't say I felt anything solid, but there was the sensation of the warmth of sunshine against my skin. Rhys smiled down at me and caressed my face; it felt like the passing of a gentle breeze.

"How I have missed you Constance, who surpasses Helen of Troy and the goddesses of old in beauty. And you still knew who I was even as a tree! I would never have dreamed you'd ever come. But to come on today of all days! It is the Summer Solstice, all the gateways are open today The World of Faerie holds a strong sway over the World of Men making the impossible possible."

'Aragorn' scowled and I thought he was going

to snatch me from beside Rhys once more, but he simply hovered just behind my shoulder. "But that spell should have sealed your soul and voided your powers- an eternity of awareness with no way to ever interact."

"As it turns out, even being on Hawthorn Ringed Land on a Solstice wasn't enough to compensate for me not being a Master Wordsmith. Not to mention the last time that Heavenly Word of Power was cast, all seven living Master Wordsmiths were incanting together. I simply wasn't powerful enough to fully complete the incantation properly. But I am flattered you give me so much credit Your Highness."

I whirled around to face the very put out 'Aragorn'. "Your Highness?"

Raijin, who had billowing clouds of white hair and eyes like storm clouds spoke with a voice that rolled like thunder. "The one you named Aragorn is Kay Lyon, the Lost Elven Prince."

Rhys's one eyebrow raised. "I believe he is known as Kay Lyon, the Disgraced Elven Prince in the World of Faerie."

A new voice of an older female spoke, "I believe, oh sacred tree spirit, that you know my great nephew was falsely accused of his treason."

I turned to see a beautiful woman with ruddy sandstone skin and long, intricately braided, hematite hair wreathing her head. Though her appearance was ageless, she seemed to wear the age of the earth itself with great grace and majesty. Her noble carriage and dominate presence left no doubt in my mind as to her identity.

"Matilda?"

The elegant woman's lips slightly turned up at one corner as a sparkle took up residence in her eyes. It was a look that made me think she knew all the secrets of the universe and enjoyed watching everyone else scrambling to find them.

"That is not my given name, but it suits me well enough. I've grown rather accustomed to it. Which is just as well, for there are few who know the tongue of my given name in the Twin Worlds."

I whipped my head around to see if Nerida was . . .

Standing next to a very bumfuzzled Vidette was a gracefully lithe but powerful looking young woman with blue roan waves of hair, whose eyes glittered as with sunlight off a placid lake. There was something about her that was at once gentle and dangerous. As she smiled at me I got the sensation of watching sleepy waves lapping the shore and knowing they were full of the potential to become a tsunami.

"Nerida, has been my name since I have forsook the name given to me by my family; whom I have disavowed and who has disavowed me."

A voice spoke that sent a chill down my spine.

"All you legendary fair folk and none of you paying the slightest of attention to what is important."

Something pulled me backward and I felt a strange sensation of passing through time and space. Whatever had pulled on me did not have the ability to hold onto me and I stumbled out of the Hawthorn Gate onto an unknown forest floor.

Behind me came a pile of bodies beneath which a I barely managed not to be crusshed. It took some time for Vidette and my supposed horses to un-tangle themselves.

Rhys appeared by my side, "Constance are you hurt? What are you playing at Eagan?"

Rhys ferocity was such that he almost took on a fully corporeal form. The tree spirit Eagan only laughed. With an effervescent form that was as cold as Rhys was warm, Eagen still maintained a spiteful air about him.

"Well, everyone was trying to impress Con-stance and no one noticed I was even there, so I thought why not cause a bit of trouble."

"Well at least you've been of some use you wicked boy," a grizzled voice grumbled. "Con-stance you forgot this."

I turned to see two more figures appear in the forest out of the Hawthorn Gate. The first was a man with a shaggy beard and hair that reminded me of a gunmetal grey haystack offering me my journal.

"Chaucer!?! Then does that mean . . ."

Giggling, the second figure flew on glittering wings. She had butterscotch hair and oversized lavender eyes. "Yep, I'm Beatrix. We never knew my given name, my parents were lost to the Foul Ones when I was a baby; Chaucer found me and took me in just before he escaped to the World of Men."

Out of the corner of my eye I saw Vidette shoot me a look of bewilderment mixed with mild alarm. "So wait a minute are we . . ."

"Precisely my dear Vidette we are in the World

of Faerie. And it is about time. I have now with me heirs of the Element of Fire (he pointed to 'Aragorn' who was really Kay Lyon), the Element of Water (he pointed to Nerida), the Element of Earth (he pointed to Matilda), the Element of Wind (he pointed to Raijin), and a Child of Magic (he pointed to Beatrix). Plus twin sacred spirits who can command the power of words, the heir apparent of the Chief Elder Sage, and a 777th generation Dreamcatcher destined to rival her Spiritwalker ancestors of old. And then me, a wizard so old I don't remember my own given name. Do you have any idea how long it has taken me and to what lengths I have had to go to assemble such a fellowship?"

My admiration for Vidette's spunk only grew as she quipped, "Please don't tell me you have a ring we have to throw in a volcano. I am not really wearing the proper shoes for a yearlong wandering hike in the wilds of the World of Faerie."

I thought the old wizard who was once Chaucer the Canterbury Bunny would scowl, but he only laughed. "Oh, Tolkien. I did love that man for his ability to endear the hearts of the World of Men to the fair folk of the World of Faerie. Tolkien and Lewis both. Now there were a pair of Master Wordsmiths to be sure. Oh, the shenanigans and adventures those two would get up to! But no my dear Vidette, I've a much more weighty matter in need of those with superlative qualities such as yourselves. But for now, I think we best find us a place to make camp away from eyes that could get us into trouble."

We've done little more since arriving other than trying to get the measure of one another, find a place to sleep, and procuring food. I have so many questions in my mind. How do the Faerie come to have the forms they do in the World of Men? How do they perceive the world in those forms? How did they come into the care of the Hawthorn Wordsmiths? How did the solstice and the presence of the Hawthorns let them take on their true forms? And most importantly, what are Vidette and I going to do with our completely impractical clothing?

Well I actually got an answer to that last one. It turns out that Thrice Faerie Spelled fabric can become anything you need it to (which is why, thankfully, all of the menagerie was fully clothed when taking humanoid forms). Vidette and I were unaware that our dresses, shoes, and jewelry were of Thrice Faerie Spelled magic, and we were quick to change out of our ruffles and frills into something more appropriate for adventuring. Thrice Faerie Spelled jewelry has the same properties, and our jewelry could be turned into weapons and other helpful tools.

I find it highly suspicious that we were so well prepared for an adventure in the World of Faerie. To quote Barron, somthing smelled fishy. I have to wonder if Pippa actually planned for our clothes and jewelry to be Thrice Faerie Spelled or if it was someone else. Given his behavior since our arrival, Chaucer also seems like a candidate for making such provisions.

This whole day . . . My head . . . It is safe to say I am in a world where I don't even know which

way is up, or if I can even use the perspective defi-
nitions of the World of Men. So, to recap what I do
know even if I don't understand it. This morning
I was just Constance Peters. This afternoon I was
the maid of honor at Pippa and Barron's wedding.
This evening I was kidnapped and dragged into
the World of Faerie by the tree spirit who was once
the man who tried to kill me. I was followed by
my best friend and the menagerie of animals I've
been taking care of for three years. I knew my best
friend was the heir apparent of the Chief Elder
Sage. I had no idea my horse was an outlawed
Elven prince; that he and the rest of the his herd
were all Elemental Heirs; that my rabbits are a
grumpyish old wizard and his fairy ward; or that
the man who confessed his love to me is a sacred
tree spirit.

And let's not forget, I am Faerie Kin- a Dreamcatcher. From what I've been able to wheedle out
of Beatrix, Dreamcatchers are descendant of Spiritwalkers (those beings whose souls can leave their
bodies behind and can traverse the infinite planes
of reality). Dreamcatchers can visit the dreams of
others. Strong Dreamcatchers can become Dream-
casters allowing them to communicate through
dreams at will. But the most powerful ones are
Clairvoyants, and can visit the souls of others in
waking visions by concentrating on them, giving
them the ability to see and experience what the
other person is seeing and experiencing. And to
top it all off, I am a 777th Generation Dreamcatcher, an heir to the powers of the Spiritwalkers who
have existed from the birth of the Twin Worlds.

Yep. I am going to need a new journal.

Find File # 611370
for additional information
regarding reports of
global disturbances in

the last 18 months

Acknowledgements

Huge thanks to those who lent their talents to this project.

To Mandy for preliminary edits.

To Kalyn for his final proofing, great critique, ideas, and encouragement.

There is no way to express my thanks for the passionate and wonderful work by Jessica Madorran on the cover art!

And especially to my geriatric laptop that stuck this one out with me even though we were sure it was going to die or that I'd go crazy waiting for its snail pace to catch up to my creativity. Fortunately the former didn't happen and I've been the Mayor of Crazy for some time now.

A.R.Sprouse

Armed with a Bachelor of Fine Arts in Theater from the College of the Ozarks and a Master of Letters in Visual Culture from the University of Aberdeen (in Scotland), A.R. Sprouse is a true Creative. You will find her creating no matter where she is or what she is doing.

Professionally speaking, A.R.Sprouse is a voice actor with her heart set on being a cartoon voice when she doesn't grow up. Her adventures as an author started with her first fantasy fiction novel Guardian Alva: Awakening.

www.ingramcontent.com/pod-product-compliance
Lightning Source LLC
Chambersburg PA
CBHW020247130626
46549CB00005B/2102